Through Blind Eyes

Written By: Bobbie Bean

Synopsis

Chrissy Marlow suffers a tremendous loss as a young child. She spends the rest of her days holding on to anything and anyone she loves, whether or not that love is reciprocated. She journeys through life surrendering to the will of her oppressor, subjecting her body to multiple partners, multiple beatings, and multiple heartaches. As if the external infliction was not enough, her body turns on her, forcing her to face a demon no woman wants to face. A battle ensues in Chrissy as she searches for peace, the very thing she rejects. Conflicted in mind, body and spirit, she continues to fight and raise her children the best she knows how seeking God in the Devil's playground.

Through Blind Eyes is a story about one woman's journey, a story that has no ending but just is.

Library of Congress: Catalogue-in-Publication Data, available upon request

ISBN: 9798645176037

Printed in the USA

Bobbie Bean Publishing LTD

www.bobbiebean.com

Editor: Brandi Jefferson

Cover Photo: Fred Everett

Graphic Design: Alyse Palphini | Betesboss.com

Dedication

This book is dedicated to my beautiful and loving children, Tourré Patterson, Cire Patterson, Hezekiah Patterson, Christian Patterson, Geneva Patterson, and to my beautiful parents, Barbara Mayo and George Mayo (Rest in Heaven, Dad); and to my friend Amy Lovett (Rest in Heaven). -Christine Mayo

This book is dedicated to My Morning Sun, My Cup of Tea, My Shining Star, the Best of Me, Myshon Hudgies. -Bobbie Bean

Table of Contents

Chapter 1: Boyfriend

I had seen this guy around for the past year. He used to date my next-door neighbor. She and I weren't cool, so I never knew much about him. We never really spoke, maybe a head nod or wave here or there. He was just the boyfriend next door. When I was 17, embarking upon my senior year in high school, that changed.

Late June 1991, my nephew Georgie came to live with my family and me. He had gotten into some trouble and was hanging with the "wrong crowd." My sister thought he needed a change of scenery. She thought he would do better and finish high school strong if he came to school with me. She was justified in her thinking. My nephew and I were tight. We were the same age. So surely, the two of us would drive one another to achieve greatness during our senior year. Only truth be told, we both just wanted out. Greatness was not on our list of things to do.

Nonetheless, we convinced my sister otherwise so that we could live together. That was my Georgie. I couldn't wait to have him around all the time.

Seeing Georgie and me together wasn't unusual when we stayed in separate homes. Now that we were under the same roof, we were practically inseparable.

One day, the doorbell rang. To my surprise, it was the boyfriend next door. Before I could ask what he wanted, Georgie emerged from his bedroom and introduced him as his good friend Aaron. The funny thing is I never noticed how fine Aaron was when he was next door. Now that he was up close and personal, all I could say was, damn!

Aaron had dark, rich, smooth chocolate skin. He was six feet tall. He had played sports his entire life, and when I tell you, you would know by just looking at him. Let's talk about his body! His body was banging. He wasn't big on style, but that was fixable. I mean, anything looked good on that body, and nothing, looked even better, but we'll revisit that later, not to mention that smile. I had to catch myself from falling right then and there.

Well, in usual fashion, Georgie and I continued to hang. So then, there were three — Georgie, Aaron, and me.

One day, I let Georgie keep my car while I was at work. He showed up with Aaron and another friend of his to pick me up when my shift ended. For some reason, they all felt the need to come inside my job to get me. As we walked to the car, I felt a pat on my butt. With a snap of the neck, I turned quickly to see who dared to violate me, in traditional black girl fashion.

Aaron quickly pointed to his boy, and said, "He did it!" and flashed his sinister smile. His boy pointed back at him, in adamant protest.

I knew who'd done it, and in typical black girl fashion, when I realized it was Aaron, I did not mind. I gave him a shove, that one flirty shove. When my hand hit that hard body, I could no longer fight the attraction. I liked his swag, and he was bold. He wasn't afraid of me like most boys were. He was bad, always starting and ending shit, but he was sweet to me.

Aaron always paid me compliments and let me know he wanted me. I think this had such a tremendous impact on me because I never heard it from the most important man in my life, my father. It wasn't because he didn't think I was pretty, or because he was afraid that it would go to my head, it was because he couldn't see for himself.

My father was blind. My mom was, too. I never heard, "Baby, you look beautiful in that dress... Baby, I love your hair," from either of them. I heard I was beautiful, but not that I looked beautiful. When boys said it, it didn't mean much of anything. They all wanted something from me. So, was I beautiful? Was it just my light skin and "good hair" that got the attention? I was the mixed girl on the block, the original Becky with the good hair. I remember thinking *try combing this hair. Go two days without washing this hair and tell me if you feel the same way.* Anyway, I digress. Was I really beautiful? Aaron thought so. Although he wanted the same thing every other boy wanted from me, it felt different with him. He looked me in my eyes and told me I was beautiful. He saw ME and told me I was beautiful.

For the next couple of months, I stayed with my two favorite guys. The three of us kicked it. We rolled through the parties together, we skipped school together, and we hung at the arcade. We were the clique. I felt like Aaron and I were Bonnie and Clyde, and Georgie was Clarence Clay.

It was September of '91. School had just started, and we'd finally made it to the weekend. It was time to celebrate our moment of freedom. We drove to the liquor store. I remember asking Aaron to grab me a bottle. I reached into my pocket to retrieve a couple of dollars, but before I could, Aaron was out the car saying, "I got you, ma!"

See, that was the thing about Aaron. When I was with him, I felt important. I felt protected. I felt safe. These were feelings that I rarely felt after my brother's death left me with only my blind parents to care for me. I longed for those feelings. I mean if someone ever broke in our house, who had the advantage? If a fire broke out, who had to get whom to safety? I had to be the protector due to my parents' disability, so to experience that other side again was intoxicating.

After that trip to the liquor store, it was on. We got back to my house. I grabbed Aaron's hand and waved at the ex-girlfriend next door on the way in.

We'd reached the stairs leading to my bedroom. With every step, I removed a piece of clothing. By the time we reached the top of the stairs, I was completely naked. Aaron grabbed me. He pushed me against the wall and used his pelvis to pin me in place while his tongue penetrated my ear. He whispered, telling me how bad and how long he had wanted to taste me. He continued to trace my body with his tongue, traveling from my ear to my neck. He grabbed both breasts and sucked them as if he was thirsty and in need of Vitamin D. He dropped one hand below my waist and began to spread my lips. He stroked my pearl tongue until I exploded. I didn't know it, but I had never had an orgasm before. I thought I had peed on myself. When I bust, he took his middle finger and plunged it deep in my peach. Upon extraction, he licked the sweet juices off his finger.

I thought I would pass out. My legs were trembling and writhing. I was panting like a bitch in heat. None of this stopped him. He pushed me to the bed, grabbed my hair, bent me over and commenced to drive the longest, thickest, most beautiful penis I'd ever seen, in and out…in and out…in and out of my cavity until I screamed in pleasure. He then turned me around and laid me on my back, gently. He told me he wanted to look at me while he came inside me. At that moment, I realized we weren't using a condom, but oh well …too late, now! He began to go faster and faster, harder and harder, and with one last plunge, he collapsed on top of me. I continued to release long after he was done. I had never felt anything so perfect. To this day, that was the best sex I ever had.

When I finally stopped creaming, Aaron looked at me and said, "You know we go together."

I replied, "Yes, I do."

Chapter 2: Big Bro

I really missed my brother, Georgie's dad. He was my protector when I was little. He loved me unconditionally and would kill a rock over me. Then again, he would kill a rock over much less.

My big brother was no-nonsense. He was a man of few words who brought new meaning to the phrase, “Talk to the hands.” My brother possessed a skill set that involved laying clowns down. He was a knockout artist, which came in quite handy, growing up in the projects of Queens, NY.

The streets we grew up in were like *Cheers*, that old show with the song that begins with the lines, "*You wanna go where people know the troubles are all the same. You wanna go where everybody knows your name...*" To survive in our hood, people had to know your name. People had to know you would bring trouble to whoever brought trouble to you. Well, everyone knew my big brother's name, and everyone knew my name, "baby sis."

Growing up, if anyone messed with me, I was telling my big brother. I'd run in the house crying and sick him on whomever, like a pit bull. He always went easy on the young ones. His presence alone was enough to make a kid piss his pants. He'd just tell them go on and never bother me again, and it was settled. Occasionally, those little kids had big brothers, too. You know how it is with kids, *"Well, my daddy is bigger than your daddy." "Well, my daddy can beat your daddy."* In the hood, there were more brothers than daddies to sick on each other. Therefore, when the gauntlet was thrown, big brother responded.

"Go get your big brother. I'll be right here waiting."

The other big brothers on my block wanted no parts of mine. However, you had to stand up for your family period — hood rules. So, my big bro would lay them down and repeat, "Go on somewhere, and don't bother my sister, again." He'd pick me up, put me on his shoulders, and carry me off as if I was the Queen of Sheba. That's how he always made me feel. I had my own personal bodyguard to protect me from all hurt, harm, and danger. He protected my whole family. I did not think about how that was for him, being so young with such a big responsibility. He never seemed to mind. In fact, he made it look easy. He was the man in his family, the man in our house, and the man in the streets. Unfortunately, I would learn much too soon the load he carried with such grace and tenacity.

My brother was well respected, but respect is earned not given, and, when you're the man, someone always wants to try you to gain street credibility. While certainly not the path of least resistance, this often is the quickest. So, as new faces entered the community and boys grew to men or some variation of one, more punks stepped up to get beat down.

One day, my brother got into it with this guy at his garage. He'd finished some work on his car, but the guy refused to pay what was owed. Had he known my brother, he would have known this. My brother was serious about two things — his family and his money. Messing with either one was a terrible idea. In that moment, Kanye's words of wisdom would have been very beneficial. *"You pro'lly think you could. But, uh, I don't think you should..."*

The story I heard as I sat quietly on the steps, listening to grown folks' business, went as follows.

Dude called my brother a bitch ass nigga and swung on him. My brother ducked, rolled, came back up, threw a right hook, and laid him out! My brother took the money that was owed him, threw the dude out of his garage, and simultaneously gained a new enemy. Rather than come home after this altercation, my brother continued to work. My brother took his responsibility to his customers seriously. He was so engrossed in what he was doing that he never saw his newly acquired rival coming. The dude who had been ejected from the garage just a few hours before returned, and he snuck up behind my brother. He placed the barrel of his gun to my brother's head and pulled the trigger.

When I heard this, I leaped from the spot I was in, down the stairs, startling everyone in the room. I asked, "Where is my brother?" I shouted! "Take me to my brother. Where is he? He needs me! I got to help him get better! Take me to him!"

My dad said in the most pitiful voice I ever heard come from his lips, "Chrissy, come sit on daddy's lap." I climbed up in my dad's lap.

He said, "Baby girl, you can't see your brother right now. He's sleeping. He's sleeping with the angels. You will see him again, but just not right now."

I said, "Daddy, why can't we wake him up? Or we don't even have to wake him. I just want to hug him while he sleeps."

Dad replied, "Chrissy, we can't wake him up because we can't reach him. He is in Heaven now."

My big brother, my protector, was gone. I buried my face in my daddy's chest and cried and cried. My brother was twenty-five years young, and I was nine years young, but from that moment forward, I would never be young again.

Georgie and I never got over the loss of his father, my brother, but we got through it the best we could, together. This is one reason I was always so attached to Georgie. He still allowed me to have a part of my big bro and experience that unconditional love.

I know my affinity for Aaron, stemmed from the void left by the death of my brother, as well. Aaron allowed me to feel protected and secure. The power I felt when I said, "My boyfriend is going to fuck you up," felt a lot like that feeling I experienced as a child running to get my big brother. I could never be baby sis, again, but I could be Aaron's girl, and I planned to be Aaron's girl for a long time.

Chapter 3: Stanger Danger

I didn’t know how to react the first time Aaron hit me. Was I angry enough to whip his ass? Was I happy he cared so much? Was I hurt beyond belief that he would intentionally do bodily harm to me? I mean, I had never seen my dad and mom fighting. However, my sister used to beat the brakes off her "man." Whenever I asked why she’d tell me it was because she loved him so much. She couldn’t bear to think of him with someone else. Wasn’t this the same situation? Was it my fault he hit me? After all, wasn’t I the one that put that thought in his head? Let me back up.

It was November, and Aaron and I had been together for about two-and-a-half months. We were heading to the big game, and then the after-party where we would celebrate our victory. At least, those were our intentions. Well, things didn’t go as planned. Aaron's team lost in the last minute of the game, and Aaron was devastated. It was his senior year. What football player didn’t want and expect to go out with a bang? Sure, he had already earned a full ride to just about any University in the country, but this marked the end of a legacy.

When Aaron emerged from that locker room, something felt very different. His demeanor was unfamiliar. He was so angry and aggressive. His tone, his walk, his everything was on 10,000. I'd seen him mad before, but not like this. I quickly suggested we get something to help us feel better, and the group agreed. So, Aaron, a few of his teammates, and myself headed to the liquor store. We then went to get something to smoke to take the edge off before heading to the party. We may not have been celebrating a championship, but we still had a winning season. I was proud of Aaron and wanted to show him.

We arrived late but still had plenty of time to get it in, though Aaron was in no mood for it. He was cold and standoffish, even after our smoke session. I tried lifting his spirits, pointing out his many victories, but nothing worked. After a while, I gave up. Rather than spend the rest of my night sulking, I decided to relocate to the other side of the room with my girls. There was no point in both of us letting a good party go to waste. The funny thing was that must have been Aaron's cue to turn up cause when I left, so did his nasty demeanor. Suddenly, he was the life of the party.

I remember gazing across the room only to find Aaron with girls all over him. He was smiling, laughing, dancing, and grinding — oh, what a difference three minutes, a big butt, and a smile made. Who knew? As I watched in disbelief, I thought to myself *clearly, he has lost his ever-loving mind.* I began to migrate upon him and his band of groupies, but before I reached him, something… correction, someone caught my attention. Amid my rage, I was able to pull my eyes away from Aaron long enough to notice someone noticing me. That someone was about 6'1, chocolate, with a body just how I like. He was fine, and he was right on time! No need to exert energy yelling and fighting when I could have so much fun getting even. Aaron needed to understand he was not the only boy who wanted me. He needed to know that he, too, was like a city bus…miss one, and in 15 minutes, the next one's coming.

Since turnabout is fair play, I made a point to forget all about Aaron in that hour we had left. I danced with the chocolate cutie all night. He was from the Midwest, and he had a different swag about him. He was sexy, well groomed, and smelled good. He was just in town for the big game. So, when the party ended, so could we. He was the perfect specimen for operation get even. Of course,

Chocolate Drop had something different in mind. He attempted to rewrite our ending. He invited me to hang out and hit IHOP. I told him I had a curfew, which was a lie, but he bought it. He then asked for my number. Despite the distance between us, he had people in New York and visited often. He "wanted to get to know me better." He wanted to make me his east coast, boo.

I declined. He'd served his purpose. I just needed him for one reason and one reason only, to make Aaron jealous. I was pretty sure I had accomplished that. I had yet to confirm or deny my assumption, considering Aaron and I never made our way back to each other during the party. However, if Aaron got the slightest glimpse of me, and I was certain he did, rest assure that mission was accomplished. So, when the lights came on, I was out.

I returned to the car to meet Aaron and other passengers for our journey home. I knew he wouldn't say anything in front of his boys unless I initiated the conversation. I elected not to. In fact, I wasn't going to mention his shenanigans at all. This incident called for drastic measures. Silence was my weapon of choice. My mother used to tell me if you want a man to act right, be quiet. If you are not showing your hand, hollering and hooting, and carrying on after a man has offended you, they get scared. They think you don't care. It's then and only then that they straighten up. She'd tell me, *"Try showing no emotion and watch what they do."* That's what I did. I said nothing all the way home. I simply turned the radio up and continued enjoying my night.

When we pulled up to Aaron's house, I remember Guys' "Piece of my Love" was playing. As the song began, Aaron started humming along. This dude didn't sing, so this was odd. When the song got to the part where Aaron Hall sings dumb bitch, my Aaron was all in, singing particularly loud, emphasizing the "dumb bitch." All the while, I'm wondering. When is he getting out of the car? A few minutes pass, and he still doesn't exit. He did, however, decide to break our silence.

He says, "You know that's what I tell them."

I asked, "Tell who?"

He says, "These thirsty chicks. I tell them I'm with you. I love you, so I can only fuck them. They only get a piece of my love."

I thought to myself, *surely you jest. He couldn't have said what I thought he said.* However, he repeated it. I said to myself, *OK, this how we're playing this.* I looked at Aaron, and I grabbed his hand and said, "That's why we're perfect for each other. I tell thirsty niggas the same thing. That's what I told dude I was dancing with."

Aaron looked at me.

"What did you say?"

I replied, "I tell thirsty niggas the same thing. I'm with someone, but you can have a piece."

Aaron rotated his wrist to grab my arm. He squeezed it so tight as he pulled me closer. He balled up his free hand into a fist, and he punched me twice in my right thigh.

What just happened? Did this nigga just put his hands on me? I contemplated swinging back, but then I realized I couldn't win. There is nothing in this car to give me any kind of chance. There is a crowbar in the trunk and a bat in the trunk, but odds of me getting to them are slim. And let's say I do get to the crowbar or bat, what are the odds of him taking them from me? I'd say, pretty good.

As these thoughts rushed through my head, I fought hard to hold back my tears. My leg was throbbing, but I couldn't continue to show weakness. I mustered up enough strength to pull my arm away and told him to get out of my car. He refused. Instead of getting out, he started grabbing on me and telling me how sorry he was. He kept trying to kiss me. I continued to struggle and pull away.

I just kept saying, "Get out. Get out!"

Finally, he did, but he didn't leave. Instead, he ran around to my side of the car. I was so discombobulated that I couldn't lock the door fast enough. He pulled me out of the car, and I knew he was about to beat my ass. He threw me against the hood of the vehicle, and by this time, I'm swinging, but in vain. Not one hit slowed him down. He lifts me off the ground, sits me on the car, constrains me with one hand, and pulls my pants down with the other. He starts to play with my clit as he speaks softly.

"I never tell girls that. I just wanted to make you mad for dancing with that nigga. You know you the only one for me, and I didn't mean to hit you that hard. You know I'd never hurt you," as he plunges his finger deep inside me. "I know you ain't told nobody they can have a piece of you. You know better. This is my pussy."

By this time, I've fallen under his spell. I'd forgotten that I wouldn't be able to wear shorts for months. Good thing it was fall, nearing winter.

He asked me, "Is this my pussy?"

"Yes, it's your pussy," I replied. He then let go of my arms, wrapped both of my legs around his head, and licked until I melted all over the hood of my car.

Chapter 4: Love Hurts

The next morning, I woke up in pain. I had a huge contusion where Aaron punched me. As I lay there, considering the right thing to decide, the phone rang. It was Aaron, calling to see how I was feeling. I told him I was wounded. He said he'd be right over with ice packs and things he kept in stock to ease the pain from his own battles on the football field. Who better to treat my wound than someone who was accustomed to getting hit by men his size on a regular?

I remember hearing the doorbell ring. I immediately felt butterflies, or were they moths? I couldn't tell. I didn't know if I was excited or nervous, and not the good kind of nervous, but the scary kind. Did I want to run to him or from him? I really didn't know. I remember it like it was yesterday. My dad answered the door.

"It's me, Big G."

"What's up, Aaron? Sorry about the game last night, how are you feeling?"

"I'm cool," Aaron replied.

"It was rough. But hey, you win some, you lose some."

"And you make 'em pay, either way, right son?"

"Yes, sir!"

"Did you hurt somebody?"

"You know me! You know I did that, Big G!"

I wonder what my dad would have said had he known that someone he hurt was me. I wonder what my dad would have felt if he could see the massive bruise on my thigh. I wonder what that conversation would have sounded like, then.

This whole ordeal was quite surreal. Aaron had some nerves coming to my house as if nothing happened. He had a conversation with my dad as if he hadn't just violated his daughter in many ways, just a few short hours prior. I think I was more offended by their exchange than the actual act. Did he think I forgave him because he made me cum? That moment of weakness certainly didn't constitute forgiveness and certainly didn't warrant him coming in my house with no shame. I know I played a part in his delusions of grandeur. I should have resisted. There was just something about him...something that I found quite irresistible.

Aaron was skilled. I don't know if I was inexperienced or if he was over experienced, but he used to make me go crazy. He used to relieve me of all scruples and all inhibitions. Still, this certainly put a damper on things. I don't care how good the dick and tongue were. How could I be ok with this? How could I let him hit me then have me? What was I thinking? We've been "together" all of two months, and he feels he can put his hands on me! If my brother were still here, he'd be dead. However, he's not, and it's a good thing. My brother would have overreacted. I mean, if Aaron really wanted to hurt me, he would've aimed for my face or my stomach, or something, right?

Aaron finally made his way up the stairs. With every step, the flutters in my stomach increased. As he breached my doorway, a delightful smell filled my room. Along with ice packs, he brought flowers, my favorite colors at that. They were pink and purple and matched my room. He was so thoughtful at times. Unfortunately, I quickly learned those thoughtful times usually followed indiscretion.

Nevertheless, those times are what made me love him. I think Pac said it best, *"I'm a sucka for love."* Yeah, I was most definitely a "sucka for love."

Aaron placed the flowers on my nightstand near our picture and then kissed me on my forehead before taking a seat next to me. He repositioned me on the bed so that I could rest my leg on his thigh. He raised my pant leg to examine the bruise. He began to shake his head back and forth, telling me he can't believe he did that. He never meant to hit me that hard. He kissed my thigh and then administered aid by icing it. He also played Benson. He did not want me going up and down the stairs. He wanted me to rest my leg so that it could heal faster. He made our lunch, and he waited on me hand and foot. If I didn't believe him before, I did now. He was genuinely sorry. He really didn't mean it, and he loved me.

Aaron hung out the whole day. Around seven, we decided to watch a movie, so he carried me downstairs to watch the big TV. My parents usually passed out at seven o'clock every night. My nephew ran the streets every night, so we pretty much had the living room to ourselves. Aaron gave me a blanket, made us popcorn, and held me.

We made it through about an hour of *The Five Heartbeats* when Aaron's beeper started going off.

"Who is that?" I asked.

He replied, "It's just my mother."

"You can call her. The phone is right there."

"Nah, I know she just wants something from the store, and I'm not ready to go."

"What if it's important?"

"If it's important, she would have paged me 911. I'm cool. We're cool. Watch the movie."

That pager never stopped going off, and he never returned the call. Later, I'd find out why, but right then, in that moment, I was good.

* * *

The next morning, I woke up in the same spot Aaron left me, but when I opened my eyes, Aaron was not there, Georgie was. He was just staring at me.

“Georgie, why are you staring at me like that? What’s wrong with you?”

“A better question is what’s wrong with you?” Georgie replied.

“What do you mean?” I asked.

“Why do you have a massive bruise on your leg? What happened? I asked my boy before he left up out of here. He gave me some lame response claiming not to know. He claimed you were just clumsy and didn’t know how you got that bruise. I don’t believe that. How do you not know where you got a bruise like that? What really happened?”

“Georgie, I don’t even know what you are talking about right now. Give me a minute to wake up.”

“You don’t need to wake up to tell me what happened. Just keep talking. What happened to you? I know that nigga ain’t put his hands on you. I know that nigga ain’t touch my blood. I don’t give a fuck how cool we are. That ain’t gon’ neva be all right. So, what happened?”

I was so glad my nephew went off on that tangent because he gave me time to come up with an excuse. If I told him what really happened, no question, he was going to see Aaron. One of them would have ended up dead because both were crazy. Besides, Aaron proved to me that he was genuinely sorry. He took such good care of me. He wouldn't touch me again. I wasn't going to break up a friendship and start a war over one mistake. I would not choose between my blood or my love.

"Georgie, you know Aaron wouldn't touch me. I got drunk Friday night and stumbled into the edge of the car door. That metal hurt so badly that I was paralyzed for about two minutes."

Good answer, I thought to myself. Anyone who has felt the edge of a car door knew what kind of damage it caused. That should put an end to the interrogation.

Well, the interrogation did end, but the suspicion did not. Georgie continued to look in my eyes as if he was staring his way to my soul. Finally, he spoke up.

"Chrissy, if ANY man ever put his hands on you, you know what would happen, right?"

I said, “Of course, Georgie.”

He said, “Ok! I don’t care who. I don’t care why. I don’t care when.”

“I know, Georgie.”

“I love you, Auntie,” he said, smirking. We thought it funny to call one another auntie and nephew because we were so close in age.

“I love you too, nephew. Now, leave me alone so that I can go back to sleep. My head is pounding.”

I closed my eyes, pretending to go to sleep, but my mind would not allow. Georgie’s words consumed me. I swear. I felt like my brother was sitting in front of me, chastising me, when he was speaking. He was so upset. Perhaps, I should be more concerned. Maybe I should slow this down, I thought, but I loved Aaron so much. I loved being Aaron’s girl.

I was so glad I never had to explain any of this to my parents. This was the first bruise they never saw, but it certainly wasn’t the last. Many times, for me, I thought blindness was a blessing. You know the saying ignorance is bliss. Well, that saying was a similar concept with regard to blindness for me. However, instead of blindness, being bliss, the blindness was secret. Blindness allowed me to stay hidden and not face my conscience.

Chapter 5: Time Heals

The declaration, “Time heals all wounds,” really does hold true. After a month or so, no sign of Aaron ever touching me remained. As he promised, he hadn’t hit me again. In fact, Aaron was nice, sweet, and attentive. Everything I wanted and needed him to be. I’m still amazed at how little we argued, considering how much time we spent together, but that’s just how it was. We were cool with each other. Georgie succumbed to time’s healing power as well and was no longer suspicious of Aaron. He concluded I was telling the truth and that the car door was the guilty party that dreadful night. Therefore, the three Amigos were back in stride again. All was well with the world and remained so for some time.

On Valentine’s Day, Aaron gave me a giant Teddy bear, which he presented to me at school. The bear was pink, fluffy, and so beautiful that I didn’t notice it was wearing a locket until Aaron removed the necklace from the bear and placed it around my neck. He kissed me gently on my collarbone, and as he whispered, “Happy Valentine’s Day” in my ear, my body began to quiver. This was probably the only time in history I was glad to be on my period. If I hadn't had that pad on, I would have leaked excitement all over my leg. I was in awe. Had Aaron really presented me with the bear and a locket with a picture of us inside, in front of the whole school? Yes, he did that! And, why wouldn't he? After all, we were high school royalty. He was the star athlete and bad boy, and I was wifey. We warranted an audience.

After this magnificent display of affection, Aaron turned and headed toward class. The entourage dispersed. There I was speechless and wet. When I finally snapped out of the enthralled state he left me in, I realized I too had to get to class. My bear would not fit in the locker, so he stayed by my side for the rest of the day. I felt like I was the baddest chick in the building! My friends could tell me nothing, that day.

* * *

Summer arrived, and our senior year had finally come to an end. I was Howard bound and proud. Aaron was being scouted by schools all over the country. When he decided on Cincinnati, I was taken aback. He was supposed to stay close. We were supposed to visit one another on the weekends. I was still supposed to go to his games, rocking his jersey. The distance from Washington, DC to Cincinnati, Ohio would foil that plan.

After an invitation and a little consideration, I decided Howard was not as important as Aaron was. I was going to UC so that Aaron and I could be together. Georgie did not agree with my decision. Aaron was his boy, and Georgie knew he would be challenging to manage in college. He felt like we should go our separate ways, and if meant to be, we'd find our way back to each other. This was one of those times I felt my brother's spirit had invaded his son's body to communicate with me. I saw and heard my brother say, "*Chrissy, you must live for you. Pursue your own dreams. Don't lose sight of your goals, chasing someone else's.*" Conversations like this made me realize how wise Georgie was. He was wise far beyond his years. Of course, I did not listen. I understood and appreciated what he was saying, but I did not listen. Aaron and I were in love and destined to be together forever. At 18, though? What can I say? When I was a child, I spoke as a child. I understood as a child. I thought as a child. I had yet to become a woman and put away childish things.

Chapter 6: Thick As Thieves

Aaron, Georgie, and I were thick as thieves, and I mean that literally. That's what we did for fun. We were thieves, and we would steal. Since we needed money for school and knew what our parents could give us would not be enough, we were going to take matters into our own hands. We were going to step it up a notch. What was once done for part-time fun would become full-time work.

Aaron and Georgie were the boosters, and I was the getaway driver. Now, be clear, there were never any firearms or weapons involved, just cuffing. Aaron and Georgie were pros, stealing clothes, diapers, bottles, formula, baby wipes, soap, detergent — whatever the hood needed. They stole alcohol so that we could supply our underage counterparts. Yes, the law of supply and demand was in full effect. The people got what they needed and wanted at an affordable price. We got we needed to line our pockets as we journeyed off to school. In our minds, a win/win situation had ensued. We knew we were being stupid, especially with Aaron's scholarship on the line and my college career ahead. However, when you're young, dumb, and broke, stupid makes enough cents to make sense.

One day, I got bold. I decided to journey over to the darker side. I wanted a specific outfit for my first college party. I couldn't rely on Georgie and Aaron to pick out what I wanted. I had to handle this one myself. So, the three of us went into this little hip-hop style boutique inside of the hood mall.

Now, when stealing from the hood mall, one had to be as concerned, if not more concerned with the owners of the stores as they were the cops. The owners stayed strapped and were ready to defend what they'd worked for. As we neared the entrance to the boutique, I hoped and prayed the owner was not there. When I stepped inside and found my prayers had been answered, I had all the confidence in the world. I was ready to load up. I was fearless!

I began to grab any and everything I liked in duplicates and triplicates. My philosophy was, "The more I grabbed the harder for them to detect the thing that is missing." I went into the dressing room with my arms full. I knew my size, and I knew how the clothes fit. So, rather than try the clothes on, I simply sifted through the clothes to retrieve the correct sizes.

I was happy to discover the pants I'd picked up were indeed exactly what I had envisioned for my first college party outfit. The shirts, on the other hand, were not. They were cute, but not quite right for that party outfit. Nonetheless, they, too, were leaving with me.

I rolled everything tight and began stuffing the items in inconspicuous places on my body. I made sure everything I wanted was securely and discretely tucked before exiting the dressing room. My adrenaline was pumping. I was scared and excited at the same time, as I appeared to confidently approach the dressing room attendant to return the items I did not want. With conviction, I expressed my disappointment having not found that "just right" outfit. She apologized and wished me better luck in the next store. I motioned to Aaron and Georgie, who were "innocently" perusing the store, letting them know I was unsuccessful in finding what I wanted and was ready to leave.

Aaron and Georgie quickly joined my side, grinning, knowing I'd found plenty. We started toward the exit, but then, something caught my eye. How did I miss that? There in front of us was the shirt I wanted. Something told me, *"Keep moving. Don't be greedy. You're almost home free!"* I ignored the advice.

I whispered to Aaron, "There it is! I don't know how I missed it before, but I have to have that shirt."

He casually stopped and pretended to point something else out to me. He quietly told Georgie to reposition himself to obstruct the view of the table. I stayed by Aaron's side, pretending to admire the piece he showed me until he said go. I walked back over to the table, Aaron followed, shielding me from view so that I could snatch the item I wanted. I grabbed it, tucked it under my shirt, and continued toward the door. The next thing I knew, a security guard was standing in front of me asking me to follow him to the office.

I asked, "Why?"

He replied, "You know why… ma'am! The police are on their way. How do you want to handle this?"

Aaron and Georgie slid out of the store undetected before the real cops arrived, but assured me, they had me. “Don’t worry!” They mouthed to me. I couldn’t believe this was happening. I was going to jail.

Chapter 7: Babies & Fools

My father always told me God takes care of babies and fools. In this case, I was both, and I sure hoped my dad was right. Here I was, preparing to embark upon what was supposed to be the most exciting time of my life, yet I was facing jail time. Rather than stay at home to ponder my fate, I started college, despite what was looming overhead. I had not determined whether this act would constitute cruel and unusual punishment, a teaser that would haunt me for months to come while being confined to four walls, or if it was my mom's faith in action.

It turns out my mom's faith was in action. God found mercy on me, as did the courts. When I returned home from school for that first visit, I discovered the charges had been dropped. The police did something wrong with the arrest, and this baby fool was handed her freedom papers. I promised God, if He got me out of that jam, I would never steal again. I never did. That was a promise I would always keep.

* * *

The University of Cincinnati surprised me. Aside from the band playing “Flight of the Bumblebee” rather than “Too Legit to Quit”, UC resembled an HBCU in the partying sense. The school was segregated, not by force but because it mimicked the city. Whites hung with whites. Blacks hung with blacks. Hispanics hung with blacks. With everyone else, it could go either way. Blacks had a very dominant presence on campus. The black cultural center was at the center of the campus, and the head of that sector made sure the university catered to us, as well.

The black Greeks also had a strong presence. While white Greek fraternity and sorority houses lined the college strip, black Greek frat and sorority houses lined the surrounding hoods. We had events galore on and off-campus. We had step shows, spoken word, gospel concerts, comedy shows, and plays. There were clubs in every direction that catered to the black college agenda. And the parties, the parties were off the chain! Every day of the week, we had something to do other than study.

Since I had already prepared myself to be in a partying environment, the party life did not impact me so. I mean, this was not my biggest distraction. Aaron was my biggest distraction. From the moment we touched down in Cincinnati, Aaron became estranged to me. We were never together during the day. He attributed that to class and football. We never attended any events together. Again, he attributed that to football. The guys were bonding. They were all going together, so no girls allowed. If somebody had beef with somebody else, it would get rowdy. I heard excuse after excuse during the short time I would see him, which was at night. I would have lost my mind if not for the fact I was in his bed just about every night.

At least this gave me some sense of comfort when I was told, "Just go with your girls." Every time I heard this, I would cringe as I thought to myself, *what girls? I made the trek to Cincinnati with you.* Had he forgotten that already?

Aaron did have a roommate, and the roommate had a girlfriend. They, too, were from the east coast. We all hit it off well. I mean if we were going to be in such close quarters, what choice did we have? The guys could not come to our dorms at night because they were football players with curfews. So, we had to stay with them or risk someone else being in their beds at night. Neither of us was having that. So, when Aaron and his roommate were out gallivanting, she and I were left to talk. She and I became what I thought would be friends, but that didn't really pan out. She rarely went anywhere or did anything. She'd just sit around bragging about how much money she had from modeling and how much money her family had, all while waiting on her boyfriend to come back to the room. She'd talk about how she got money from the time he left to the time he returned. Hence, we nicknamed her, "I get paid."

What's that you ask? *"Who is we?"* Oh, well, Aaron also developed a relationship with another guy on his football team. He was from the Midwest. He too had a "secret," "part-time" …however you want to coin it, girl. Her name was Bobbie, and she was from Cincinnati. She knew a few people, of course, being from that city. However, she didn't really hang with anyone from Cincinnati. She was cool with them. They just didn't hang. She was good at making acquaintances, and eventually friends, if worthy, and, only a few were worthy.

She did not use the word friend lightly. I happened to be worthy. Bobbie and I were the "we" I referred to. We dubbed ole girl, "I get paid." Come to think of it. It may have been another one of our associates who had little tolerance for her that came up with the name. Whatever the case, the name stuck.

Bobbie, "I get paid", and I hung for a bit. We shared a few moments together. I remember this chick that stayed in a neighboring dorm was allegedly messing with Bobbie's dude. She went to confront her, woman-to-woman, to ask her if she was messing with him. The girl called Bobbie out her name, and the next thing you know, Bobbie was on top of her. "I get paid," snatched Bobbie off the girl and dragged her to the next room with the strength of a man, talking about how we need not fight over dudes. We are too cute for that. What she didn't understand was Bobbie didn't fight over dudes. She was fighting because the girl called her out her name. Now, when "I get paid" went ballistic after finding out her dude was cheating on her and commenced to breaking everything in his room and sought out the girl he was messing with, that was fighting over a dude. Since misery loves company, she also revealed during that angry tirade, that Aaron was messing with her sister. That's when she and I fell out. Bobbie was team Chrissy. So, it was over for her. She lost her man and the only two girls that could stand to be around her for longer than five minutes in one sitting. Oh well, c'est la vie. She ended up packing her bags and leaving school like within a week. Aaron, of course, denied everything, and, since "I get paid" was gone, the sister became a moot point. So, regardless of whether the accusations were true, out of sight was out of mind.

Bobbie and I remained and grew tighter. We developed relationships with other football player girlfriends. Bobbie had a couple of girls she had met at orientation who were cool. Our click grew. We were from different coasts and different cities, but we were all a tad rowdy. We had fun. I had a distraction from my distraction, and I had back up when I could no longer ignore my distraction. Back up was a must because I didn't have an off switch.

When Aaron was involved, I was nuts. One time, I saw him flirting with this chick that rumors were flying around about. She had a car full of girls, and he was riding on the hood of her car as if to stop her from leaving him. They were all laughing and playing. I saw this and saw red! Bobbie tried to grab me, but she couldn't. I took off running. I chased the car down. I snatched him off the car and started whaling on him. I wasn't worried about the girls. My girls were there, so it was whatever. I was fed up.

After a few good licks, Aaron grabbed me and restrained me to stop me from swinging. He pulled me away from the crowd and dragged me behind a building. Had we been alone, I don't know what he would have done to me. We were not alone, though. Bobbie was right behind us. She let him know she was right behind us, too. At this point, she had no knowledge of him having hit me in the past. She was just shell shocked from her real-life experiences with domestic abuse and wasn't having it. She didn't agree with me putting my hands on him, either, which she adamantly expressed to me later that night. However, she was not under any circumstance going to leave me to be dealt with. Aaron cursed me, called me a few dumb bitches, and told Bobbie she'd better get me. Bobbie grabbed my arm and encouraged me to come with her. Aaron left and went on about his night, but not with those girls. As far as I was concerned, mission accomplished!

Chapter 8: Ground Zero

UC's campus became ground zero for an east coast/west coast war. Only, this time, Biggie, Tupac, the Crips, and the Bloods were not the ones at odds. The ladies ran that mutha. The east side dorm girls beefed with the west side dorm girls, all day every day. One does not have to be a rocket scientist to know why — the guys found cheating easier. Let me rephrase that. The guys were less likely to get caught cheating if the girls they messed with were from separate sides of the campus. This, of course, caused a lot of friction between the two sides. Between the dirty looks, shit talking, shoulder brushes, and dance battles, somebody was popping off every day of the week.

Now, out of all the chicks I hung with, Bobbie was the only one who did not stay on campus. She lived at home during her freshman year. No one knew she wasn't a resident but us. She was there 24/7. She went home in the wee hours of the night to sleep, but that was it. She was in the café, eating off somebody's card. She was sneaking up the stairwells to bypass the RAs, and she was winning resident Spades tournaments. She was there for it. She was part of our world, so she was part of the turf war, as well.

We had issues on and off campus with our counterparts, and I found it hard to escape. I remember the girls and I decided to sneak down to Freaknik. Well, Bobbie and I were the only ones sneaking. She was afraid to ask her mom, and Aaron was not letting me go. Therefore, I told Aaron I needed a little breather from his shenanigans and would be spending the weekend with Bobbie. Bobbie told her mom she would be staying on campus with me for the weekend, and we hit the road.

I thought summers on Jones Beach were sick, but Freaknik was the sickest ever. Imagine highways shut down for miles with parked cars on them. Every vehicle, every business, every booming system blasting R. Kelly's "Bump & Grind" and Adina Howard's "Freak Like Me" and everyone, everywhere for miles is in the streets, the parks, and the alleys, kickin' it!! Blunts were passed all around, alcohol was everywhere, and the men…fine dudes from all over wanted nothing but a minute. I had a ball! My people knew how to party.

For a couple of days, I had no cares, no worries. Finally, I was not thinking about Aaron. All I had to worry about that weekend was my girls and myself. No way would I run into him, because of football. I was good. He would never know. All was well with the universe. Then we ran into a chick from that other side of UC's campus.

I would soon find out the chick we ran into was one of Aaron's whores. At the time, I did not know. I just knew I didn't like her. I knew from the dirty looks she gave me, she wanted Aaron, but there was no way in hell he was messing with this ugly broad. She looked like a freaking 13-year-old ugly boy. Nonetheless, as soon as we saw her manly ass, Aaron began blowing my phone up.

I ignored Aaron's calls. I was not at all prepared to face this music. So, when he could not get ahold of me, he did the unthinkable. He called Bobbie's mom and snitched. Shortly after Bobbie's phone started blowing up. She answered, and her mom was pissed! Bobbie told her mom Aaron was lying. He was mad at me, and she'd be home later. We had to hightail it to Cincy after that. Our trip was cut a little short, but it sure was fun while it lasted.

Now, since Aaron couldn't tell me he was messing with that boy-girl, he couldn't really push the issue about Freaknik. I told him I was at Bobbie's the whole time and just didn't want to talk to him. Bobbie's mom co-signed. She was cool like that. He had no choice but to drop it. Unfortunately, at this point, I had to admit to myself Aaron's relationship with the boy-girl was not a suspicion but indeed a fact. Aaron must have known my spidey senses were tingling and shut things down, because I didn't catch much flak from the boy-girl after this incident. That is until I got pregnant in September of '93.

Word traveled across campus like wildfire. I was in complete and utter shock. We had been having unprotected sex for a couple of years without any scares, so I thought I could not have babies. Yet, I was expecting. I was afraid and excited at the same time. I loved Aaron to death and now I was giving him a baby. I had the upper hand on all his hoes. He really loved me, so I thought. He didn't even ask me to abort my baby. He is going to be my husband one day.

I was on a cloud for some time. Aaron was sweet to me. Rumors died down, but then I began to show. I was a little thing, so this kind of messed with my head. We were broke college students. Neither of us had money to get maternity clothes. I felt fat instead of pregnant. To add insult to injury, the boy-girl, whose name I later found out was Terri, decided to rear her ugly head once more at the most inopportune time in my life.

I was headed to the café with Bobbie, and I hear this chick talking shit behind us.

I hear this voice behind me say, "I'm going to kick her ass."

Before I could get turned around good, Bobbie was asking "Whose ass you bout to kick?"

This bitch had the audacity to say, "I'm going to kick her ass," and pointed at me.

I started to respond. Bobbie cut me off. She said, "Don't you dare work your pregnant self up. I got this."

Bobbie turned to the boy-girl and started walking toward her.

"You think you gon' fuck with her while she pregnant? Bitch, kick my ass! How bout that? Kick my ass! You ain't gon' do a mutha fuckin' thing to her! Believe that!"

The chick's friends "pulled" her back. They turned and walked away. Bobbie and I locked arms and went on to the café.

* * *

Things between Aaron and I worsened from there. I could not believe he had bitches thinking they could run up on me, and especially while carrying his child. I wonder did he hit her when he found out what she'd done. Did he grab her up and choke her up? Did he call her out her name? Did he drag her by her hair? Well, he could not have done that. She was bald-headed. Did he drag her by her arms, black her eye, or bust her lip? Did he just reserve that energy for me? I wonder.

My apologies, I digress.

Shortly after that, I went home to be with my family in Jersey. My mom could tell I was stressed. She wanted me home where I could get proper healthcare and proper treatment both physically and mentally. As much as I loved Aaron, I loved my baby more, so I went home.

It's true when they say distance makes the heart grow fonder. I received calls all the time from Aaron, saying how much he missed me being there. He said I'd been by his side so long that he didn't know how to be without me. It felt good to hear these words without interruption. I was away, so I didn't know what time he was getting back to his dorm, or who was in his bed. I couldn't see him flirting with other girls. I didn't have chicks giving me dirty looks and murmuring behind my head. All I had was his words.

"I miss you. I want you to come back to live with me when you have the baby. We'll get an apartment off-campus. I will be so much better to you and my baby than I was. I only love you."

These words resonated within my spirit.

I was happy with Aaron again. I was in a space where I could be ignorant of what he was doing, and ignorance is bliss. Then I found out the boy-girl had a whole gang of girls lined up to jump Bobbie. What she didn't know about Bobbie is, Bobbie is blessed and highly favored. She always has been. So, when you think you got her surrounded, an army comes from nowhere to fight by her side.

Bobbie was outnumbered. She was with two girls, only one of which would fight, and they were nowhere near each other. The boy-girl had a whole line of Kappa dolls, aka groupies with her. She wasn't even part of a real sorority. They surrounded Bobbie on the dance floor. The boy-girl stepped up. Bobbie drew back to swing, but before she could, a girl came from behind her and stole the boy-girl in the face. So, Bobbie ducked under her arm and grabbed the next girl in line and started beating her. It turns out the boy-girl liked bullying girls she thought couldn't defend themselves like in my case because of the baby, or who wouldn't because they were timid.

Nevertheless, a person can only take so much before they blow. That's what happened. The next thing you know, the bullied girl's roommates jumped in. They were still outnumbered, but together they wore that whole line out.

The fight spilled outside. The police came, broke it up, but at three in the morning, Bobbie, and the bullied girl's roommates were still outside waiting on the boy-girl and her clique to come back for another round. They never showed. They quickly learned they did not want it with my girl at all.

Bobbie was familiar with her newfound battalion of stallions. They were not complete strangers. She had seen them several times at Sweets' house. Sweets played football with Aaron. He was also a Kappa, and his house was the unofficial Kappa house where all the epic Kappa parties went down. Sweets and Bobbie were real good friends, so she was always there. The girls that fought alongside her that night frequented Sweets' parties as well. They would always speak to each other, but the fight led them to a sisterhood and bonds that would never be broken. Although I was ecstatic about the new friendships, all I could think of when hearing that my girl got jumped was, *I'm going to kill this bitch!*

Chapter 9: 48 Hours

I went to one Lamaze class throughout my entire pregnancy. Since Aaron was still away at school, he was unable to attend. So, of course, my ride or die, Georgie stepped in. Georgie did his best to keep me engaged throughout the class, but he could not. I was bored to tears after the first 15 minutes. We stayed until the end, but that was the first and last class I would attend before giving birth to my beautiful daughter, Sasha. You know how it is. When your young and dumb, or maybe naïve is a better term, you think you know it all. I was no different. I never picked up a book. I never talked to my elders. Instead, I sought information from the reliable source most adolescents choose, my Jersey girl, Shay.

Shay had just given birth to a beautiful baby boy, whom she was able to deliver naturally with the aid of a midwife and some birthing classes. I strongly felt I could rely on her expertise and be just fine.

Shay taught me I was already equipped with everything I needed to bring a child into this world. She said women have a high tolerance for pain and do not need medication to facilitate a successful childbirth. All the medication would do is slow the process. She even hit me with this… *"You do not want to turn your baby into a dope fiend, do you?"* That was all I needed to hear. No, I did not want my baby feening. I was convinced. I would not get an epidural. All I needed was a vagina to deliver my healthy baby, and I had one of those. I would not use drugs, nor did I need classes to do what I was created to.

Childbirth was a natural process, and I would have my child naturally. In retrospect, my lessons from Shay should not have stopped there. I should have learned breathing techniques to ease the pain and body movement that helped the baby down the birthing canal. However, I did not. I knew all I needed to know. I had a vagina, by which she would make her grand entrance. That was that.

* * *

I had gone to the hospital several times operating under the auspices of false pretenses and primarily, the notion that labor pains feel like bad cramps. I would soon find out this was a lie, and the truth was nowhere to be found in this statement. What I was experiencing was Braxton Hicks, which pale in comparison to the real thing. I would soon know what real labor pain felt like and it was unlike any menstrual cramp I had experienced. I imagine anyone subjected to the kind of pain associated with the miracle of childbirth monthly would quickly find their way to the Brooklyn Bridge and would without hesitation, jump.

On May 23, 1994, I wasn't awakened by an alarm clock, or a bird chirping in the tree outside my window, or by the sun shining through my windowpane. No, I was awakened by something I had never experienced before. A pain so intense and excruciating shot through my abdomen and sat me straight up out of my sleep. I opened my mouth to let out a scream, but no sound escaped my body. My breath was snatched, and I could do nothing but tense up and wait for the pain to subside. I knew at that moment that this was not another false alarm, and the time had come. My baby was on the way. As soon as the labor pain released me from its Kung Fu grip, I dialed Shay. I told her it was happening and to please meet me at the hospital. I woke my mom and my nephew and told them it was go-time! We were on our way.

What should have taken 10 minutes took 20 minutes due to an accident. As a result, I had the pleasure of having two more contractions in the car as they were about 10 minutes apart. I just remember being sprawled out over the back seat in sheer agony. I held on to my mom's hand through the first. She let out the howl I couldn't from the pain of me squeezing her hand so tight. She refused me her hand the second time and elected to simply stroke whatever she could reach. I was so angry that I had been lied to about what to expect. I felt so unprepared. I would've read every book and sat through every boring Lamaze class had I known this pain was so extreme.

I was so ready for this ordeal to be over, but Sasha wasn't. I wanted so badly to skip the heavy labor and just reap the reward, but like in life, this was not an option. The pain continued for 48 hours before my daughter decided to grace us with her presence. As horrifically painful this experience was, Sasha was worth it. Sasha was worth every sweat bead that poured from my scalp; every tear that fell from my eyes, and every weakness that escaped my body.

Sasha weighed seven pounds and was eighteen inches long. She had a head full of black, curly hair and beautiful caramel skin. Her eyes were shaped like almonds and were so bold and full of life. They placed her in my arms, and as she lay on my chest, a feeling more intense than any labor pain overwhelmed me. My beautiful baby girl was here in the flesh. The little thing inside me that I fell in love with from the moment she was conceived, and the little creature I sang to night after night and read to while in my womb had made her way into this world of mine. As much as I knew her and loved her, I could not have fathomed the love that I felt in this moment.

Before Sasha's arrival, I didn't own love like this. Before her, I only owned romantic love, needy love known as Eros love and Phileo, the friendship, and parental love. But this...this was different. This was love in its purest form. This was unconditional, unwavering, never-ending love. This was agape love, the love I was told God had for me but never quite believed.

Consequently, this was the first time I truly saw who He is. I was familiar with this all-seeing, all-knowing, all-powerful being that even trumped Santa Claus. I even prayed to Him a time or two, maybe three or fifteen, if you count the arrest, but that didn't mean anything. For me, prayer was more like a shot in the dark, a Hail Mary that I was willing to take if it kept me out of situations like prison. So, most of my experience with Him was out of desperation, not adoration, or indirect, coming by way of my mother and father. I hadn't formally met the Man, until then.

See, I had trouble believing God really existed. See, if an all-seeing, all-knowing, all-powerful being truly existed, then why was my brother dead? Why were my parents blind? Why did so many bad things happen to so many good people? While I still had no answer to these questions, I could no longer doubt His existence. I didn't understand Him, but in this moment, I didn't need to. Every bad thing that had ever happened in my world was rectified the moment my child took her first breath outside my womb. Every emotional trauma that haunted my thoughts dissipated the moment they placed Sasha in my arms. Every agonizing pain I'd felt just moments before her arrival, was forgotten. As I held her close to me, the world around me ceased to exist. There was only Sasha. Something this perfect could only come from that omniscient, omnipotent, omnipresent being I had heard so many stories about. That agape love really did exist, for Sasha reflected it.

My love for Sasha was the closest to agape love I could achieve as a human here on earth, and I no longer needed understanding or further validation to know God was real. I felt Him in my heart, in my mind, in my spirit, and in every fiber of my being. I recognized it by the fact that my whole life, my entire world now existed in my child's eyes. And, as I gazed into those beautiful eyes with amazement, all I could see was God. *God, it's nice to finally meet you.*

Aaron met his daughter two days later. I could see in his eyes the pride and love he felt for his child. He, too, was overjoyed. He assured me he would lay down his life at any given moment to protect the two of us without hesitation. He asked me to please allow him to do that for us. He asked me once more, to join him in Cincinnati, and I agreed. I stayed home long enough to completely heal and until my daughter had gotten through her initial doctor's visits. Then, she and I hightailed it back to Cincinnati.

Chapter 10: Home Is Where The Heart Is

My return to Cincinnati was a far cry from what I expected and from what I anxiously anticipated. I thought things would be different, uncomfortable, and awkward. I thought my single, free friends would shy away from dirty diapers, messy feedings, and the verbal communication that consisted of cries, whines, and coos. I thought Aaron would abandon his fatherly duties upon my return, leaving me to solely manage a situation that he and I both created. I thought for certain that this could be the greatest mistake, yet, leaving the comforts of home, the support, and venturing 640 miles away to go it alone. I thought wrong.

When Aaron opened the door to our apartment and led us in, I was pleasantly surprised. I thought to myself, *wow! This is good for us.* It was large enough for us, convenient to school, and the neighbors were quiet. I don't know how Aaron managed that in a college community. He did, though, and I was happy about it.

Aaron and I worked on the nursery together. My daughter's room was pink and yellow. She had a bouncer and playpen, mobiles, and stuffed animals. My girls planned a welcome back/baby shower and got my Sasha everything she didn't have already. Bobbie and Aaron called a truce for Sasha's sake. After all, Bobbie was the godmother, so the two of them made a diligent effort to get along. She'd cook big pots of food for us so that I wouldn't have to cook. Aaron loved her cooking, especially her chili, New York-style with rice instead of spaghetti like Cincinnati does. She hated making her chili over rice but did it to appease him. It's true what they say. The quickest way to a man's heart is his stomach. Aaron stopped threatening to beat up her boyfriends. He stopped with the insults. Martin and Pam were friendly to each other, for a change. A friend of ours, Tracy, had a baby around the same time, I did. So, I wasn't the odd man out. That was a blessing. I had someone going through the same things and experiencing the same challenges as I. The two of us helped each other a lot. Life was good!

My girls and I did not miss a beat. It was like I never left. We still had our sets. We'd just pick a house and hang. Everyone would come together with the drink, the smoke, and the food. Between Tracy and Bobbie, it was going down in the kitchen, considering both were Suzy homemakers.

We'd always start with dinner, so we could get the babies fed, situated, and in bed for the night. As soon as Bobbie would finish cooking, she was taking Sasha from whoever had her. I swear I have a thousand pics with Bobbie holding Sasha, rocking her to sleep. One of the girls would be working on Tracy's daughter at the same time. The clique had a strict rule. There would be no smoking in the spot when the babies were there. So, once asleep, we'd put the babies in the bedroom with the monitors. We'd turn on some music, and head out to the patio for libations and smoke. Once we got our heads right, we'd continue the party inside. We were making this thing work!

Aaron and I alternated our nights out. This worked well for us. So, we rarely needed a babysitter. However, the night of the Euclid Ave banger, we did.

On Euclid Avenue sat a house, and the guys who lived there threw the best parties, and they never disappointed. None of the guys were Greek or played sports, so Euclid Avenue was neutral ground. They were cool with everybody. So, everybody would push through. The parties were lit. Although I was having a ball with my daughter and my girls, new and old, and life was good at home, I still had a score to settle. I hadn't forgotten what Terri did. I was not letting it slide. She still had an ass whooping coming, and I knew beyond the shadow of a doubt, she would be at that Euclid Ave party. Finally, the time had come to give her what she had been looking for, for so long.

Now, typically, the girls and I would step up in the place looking extra fly, but this night, we were on something different. Everybody had on Jodeci boots or Timbs. No one had on big earrings or loose clothes. We knew odds were that Terri wouldn't fight me heads up. So rather than kick off heels, we went prepared. I had my hair in a ponytail with no earrings. I had one mission and one only — to seek and destroy! Laura was our non-fighting friend. She remembered what happened when Bobbie got jumped, and she didn't help. So, she elected to stay home and babysit. She was a lover not a fighter. This worked out perfectly.

We arrived at the party, and I hopped out of the car like a bloodhound. I went straight in and headed to the back, no Terri. I head upstairs, no Terri. I head downstairs, no Terri. I came back up the stairs, and Terri had been spotted. I charged into the kitchen where she was. I walked up to her.

She said, "What's up?"

I said nothing. I grabbed her, snatched her out of her seat by the few strands of hair she had, and it was on. The kitchen had a door that led outside. Within a few minutes, we had wrestled our way to open space with nothing but air and opportunity between us.

My girls formed a circle around us, and I remember repeatedly, hearing Coco's voice. Coco was my new girl. She was part of the battalion that fought alongside Bobbie the night she was jumped. She was the bullied girl's roommate. Coco was from Toledo and let everyone know it. She kept a rusty box cutter on deck for whoever needed it. Her reputation preceded her. So, when she avowed, *"Anybody tries to break this up getting cut three mf'in ways."* Chicks understood her threat was not idle and stayed out of the way. My girls were not letting anyone breach the circle.

Bobbie positioned herself closest to the fight, watching every move. Anytime it looked like Terri was getting the upper hand,

Bobbie would shout out an area of vulnerability followed by instruction, "Knee her! Slam her head into that car! Head butt her!"

I followed whatever direction I was given.

I fought Terri for what felt like hours. We were on the hood of a car, and we rolled off the hood of the car. We were on the pavement. We went from the pavement to the grass and back again. This was the longest fight of my life. Finally, I kicked and clawed my way on top of Terri and wailed on her. I commenced to beating all the brakes off her.

I could hear Terri's girls trying to negotiate, asking my girls to stop the fight, to which they replied, "She asked for this. You jump in, and I'm going to beat your ass."

They were right there letting me get the justice and victory I deserved.

Terri was leaking. Still, I continued to swing with all my might. I would not stop swinging. One wrong move and I knew she could end up on top of me. I couldn't let that happen, but I was so exhausted. I kept thinking. *Please, someone, break this up!*

Bobbie saw I was on my last leg and did just that. She snatched me off Terri. Once Bobbie got ahold of me, I was able to see what I had done to Terri. I thought, *damn! I fucked her up!* My girls would never have allowed me to get beat like that, whether I deserved it or not. Oh well! She got what she was looking for.

Terri was bloody and knotted up, laid out on the pavement for her girls to scoop her. Bobbie and Coco had to literally carry me. I could not walk. My legs felt like jelly. My body felt awful, but my mind and spirit… I was so happy! And, please don't get it twisted! This was not about Aaron. Well, it was a little, but mostly, this was about the disrespect. This was about her fucking with me when I couldn't defend myself for fear of hurting my child. This was about her trying to jump my girl for stepping in like she was supposed to. Maybe if she had fought Bobbie one on one, I wouldn't have been so pressed, but to come in with 14 girls and surround her? You planned and plotted that. Since turnabout is fair play, we would have been well within our right to jump Terri, but we were not on that. We wanted our man heads up. We fought fair. I don't feel bad about what happened. I hope the bully learned her lesson. I know I had no more trouble out of her.

Laura agreed to keep Sasha for me overnight. She knew I was in no condition to get her after she heard what happened. As I made my way home, I wondered what Aaron would say. I don't know if he was at the party, but I do know he knew what went down. I turned the key and entered my home.

"Did you have a good time?" Aaron asked, sarcastically.

I replied with a resounding, "Yes!"

He then took me by the arm and led me to the tub, where he had a bath drawn for me. He slowly removed my clothes and put me in the tub. He washed my neck and gently kissed it. He gently washed my back then worked his way to the front. He dropped the sponge in the water and continued to wash me with his hands instead. I purred as he cradled and caressed my bosom with soapy hands. He rinsed them off before suckling my nipples like a baby. He hadn't really done much of that since Sasha, but tonight, we were free. I laid back in the tub, as his sudsy hands continued down my stomach and stalled at my pelvis. He parted my leaves and stroked my flower until nectar merged with the bathwater. What a way to end a great night. I slept like a baby.

Chapter 11: It Was All A Dream

I was awakened the next morning by the sound of Biggie Smalls, *"It was all a dream..."* However, it wasn't. Was it? I quickly received my answer when I attempted to jump out of bed to go to the restroom. I say "attempted" because my legs immediately gave way when I rose to my feet. My body ached from head to toe. I had bruises everywhere to the point I had to question whether I was the victor. I sauntered to the restroom and called out to Aaron to see where he was. He was in the kitchen with Sasha making breakfast. That boy sure could make some pancakes.

I watched in silence as Aaron made his way around the kitchen, feeding Sasha in between stirs and beats. I was so happy he was keeping his word by being a good father and treating me well. I had made the right decision coming to Cincinnati.

Aaron finished feeding Sasha, put her in her playpen, and then made his way to me. He placed a big plate of food in front of me, kissed me on my forehead, and said. "How you feelin', killer?"

I laughed and jokingly replied, "You should be asking your girl that," Aaron replied. "You my girl. She just sucked my dick."

Eerk! Record scratch!

For a moment, I sat dazed and confused. I was a deer, and Aaron's words were the headlights.

I regained cognizance and calmly replied, "She just sucked your dick? She just sucked your dick?"

"Chrissy, I fucked a couple of times. She used to give me money. I spent that shit on you. She just a trick!"

I was speechless. Was this Usher Raymond's "Confessions" before Usher confessed? How could he tell me any of that, and so callously?

In a matter of moments, my world crumbled. I knew Terri had liked him, but there was no way Aaron had fucked her. I wasn't fighting her for that reason. I never believed he was with her. I knew he probably got his dick sucked. I didn't expect him to tell me and have to deal with it, but he fucked her, too! He fucked with her knowing she was coming for me, disrespecting me, jumping my girl? Then, he told me. He had the audacity to let those words spill out his mouth, casually and matter of factly as if talking about something as trivial as the weather!

I continued to sit a spell, speechless until I could no longer, and then I just lost it! I threw my plate at his head with everything, including his guilt on it. I threw the glass of orange juice in his face. I called him everything but a child of God. He tried to restrain me, but there was no restraining me. I swung and swung with every ounce of strength I had left. He had the nerve to ask me why I was trippin'? Why was I trippin'? It was official. This ninja had lost his ever-loving mind.

"Why am I trippin'?"

"About something you already knew?"

"I didn't know genius! I had more faith in you than that! I thought that ugly, psycho bitch was making it up. Silly, me! Silly me to think I could trust you, the father of my child! I hate you!" He had nothing to say after that, and if he did, I wouldn't have known. I ran into our room, slammed the door, and cried.

I couldn't stop the tears, but I could start packing. So, that's what I did. I was taking my baby and getting as far away from Aaron as I could. I was going home. But then, amidst my tears, I realized. That wasn't enough. That was letting him off easy. After all, why should I have to raise Sasha by myself? I didn't create her by myself. She didn't look just like me. She looked exactly like her daddy. Nah, I wasn't leaving, but I would make him pay. I would get him back.

Even though my mind was made up, and I was determined to give Aaron a dose of his own medicine, I was no less hurt. The tears did not stop falling. I cried for days. I couldn't look at him. I couldn't speak to him. I was in so much pain. I was so happy when the weekend came. I let Aaron know that after all he had done, I would be spending time with my girls Friday and Saturday, and he needed to figure things out with Sasha. He humbly agreed, and I was out!

* * *

Friday night, we decided on a club in Covington called Dominique's. I can't say it was "the spot," because we had so many, but Dominique's was definitely one of them, and it used to jump. Before we went there, it was routine to follow the eight ball to another spot, the Bump. The Bump was where we got our liquor.

Rarely did we have to pay for alcohol. My girls were fine. They had dope boys and pro athletes on speed dial. They'd call one of them, tell them to meet us there with some weed, tell them what we wanted from the liquor store, and we'd be set. Needless to say, I was lit long before we got to Dominique's.

Dominique's was off the chain, as usual. The DJ had the party all the way live, but when we hit the door, it was all eyes on us. Within five minutes of our arrival, someone was buying us a round of drinks. No wonder, I mean, our clique consisted of every shade from white chocolate to mocha, and every shape was represented.

Coco, my girl from Toledo, was light-skinned and pear-shaped. She had bootie, bootie, bootie, bootie rocking everywhere, and was killing the wig game. She looked like a different person every time you saw her. Bobbie was caramel-colored and more proportioned but had titties and legs for days. She rocked her hair short and was known as the chick with the cute haircuts to those who didn't know her personally. I was fair-skinned, Coca-Cola shaped and petite. I would be considered "Becky with the 'good hair' today." Tracy was brown-skinned, thick, and voluptuous with long, thick natural hair. Sharae was dark-skinned, lean, and muscular with a bob. Even the white girl that hung with us was cute. We ran the gamut. There was a flavor for everyone to enjoy.

Once we got our drinks, we were off to the dance floor. All the DJs knew Coco and Bobbie and would spot them in the crowd. Those two would shut that dance floor down. So, as soon as our drinks were empty, someone who thoroughly enjoyed seeing them dance to "Dick In Ya Life," or "Flex" would be buying round number two. Bobbie never took more than was needed to get into the clubs. She believed that if she had to pay to drink, she didn't need to drink. I guess she was right because she left every party on tilt.

I wasn't a dancer like my girls, and we were not the clique that was attached at the hip. More often than not, you could catch me somewhere other than the dancefloor. This night was no exception, especially since I was on some revenge shit. So, Laura and I went trolling to see if Dominique's could supply my demand. I wasn't there 30 minutes when *bingo* I spotted the dude who would allow me to feel better. I found the dude who would allow me some get-back. And, there was no doubt in my mind he was the one. See, I had a type. Aaron was my type. He was chocolate, handsome, and tall with a thick athletic build, and he rocked Timbs. I'm from the east coast. That was our signature shoe. Well, this guy was chocolate, handsome, fine, sexy, and tall with a thick, athletic build, rocking Timbs. In fact, he and Aaron could have been cousins.

I caught his eye from across the room and immediately knew his type. He was used to girls throwing themselves all over him. So, I headed in his direction. When I smiled and walked past him, it threw him off, like I knew it would. He surely thought I was headed straight to him and would end up naked on his lap. He wasn't wrong. Only, he would come to me, not the other way around. He would approach me in ten, nine, eight, seven…*guys can be so predictable.*

"Excuse me, miss. Why you play me like that? You know you were supposed to stop and holla at me."

"Oh, really?" I replied. "And why is that?"

"Cause you supposed to leave with me tonight. You hurt my feelings, trying to act like you didn't know that already."

"Boy, you a mess!"

"No, no…Not, boy…" He quickly corrected me as he pulled me close and pressed his pelvis against mine. He leaned into me, kissed my neck, and said, "I'm a man."

"You can't prove that to me here. Now, can you?" I asked.

"I could, but I'm more of a gentleman than that. Let's go talk in my truck."

"Yes, let's!"

I told Laura I'd meet up with the girls later and followed my suitor out the door.

I was happy to see he'd parked somewhere slightly remote. He didn't want anyone damaging his nice truck.

He opened the back-passenger door first and turned me toward him. He kissed me, and it felt so good. He'd kissed me just right. He then lifted me and sat me in the backseat. He slid his hands under my shirt and began to play. I was scared because we were out in public. *What if one of Aaron's boys saw us?* I placed my hands atop his to stop him, but then, it was too late. Lust and passion had settled where my cares once were. I let go. He began to suck on my tits as he unbuttoned my pants. He slid his hand in gently massaging my clit before removing the pants completely. *Is this really happening?* How did he know I needed this so badly and would go so easily? He certainly made me a believer in that profundity — people come in your life for a reason, season, and lifetime. He was a reason, and I was glad he was in the right place at the right time to be my season.

Mr. Sexy parted lower lips with his fingers and tongue kissed my clit until I climaxed. He sat me up and said, "Put your finger inside you and let me taste it." I obeyed.

He guided my hand, plunging my finger in and out, and then licked my finger clean. He whispered in my ear, "You taste good," as he finger popped me more, hitting that G-spot persistently.

All inhibition flew out the window. He flipped me over and told me to get on my hands and knees. He climbed in behind me and penetrated me till I howled at the moon. This felt so good on so many levels for so many reasons.

When finished, he helped put my clothes back on.

Mr. Sexy said, "I undressed you. Let me get you back together."

I thought that was so cute. He walked me back to the spot. He asked for my number before we walked in.

"Nah. Let's leave this where it is."

Mr. Sexy refused and replied, "Here is my number. Use it!" We parted ways. I linked back up with my girls. Indeed, that was a wonderful night!

Chapter 12: No Regrets

The next day was somewhat surreal. I arose to greet the morning, the very late morning, in a better mental space. Contrary to my belief that I would die from the guilt of doing what Aaron did to me on a regular, just once, I was fine. I felt no remorse, and I had no regrets. I was peachy keen. I could look at Aaron without snarling. The sound of his voice saying, "good morning," did not send me into a complete frenzy. Who knew that old cliché the best way to get over an old man is to get under a new one, was true?

I made my way out of bed to get my day started. I went into Sasha's room to see what my little mama was up to. She was inching around her playpen, tossing her small baby blocks around, just as innocent and free. She was so beautiful and so sweet. Her eyes lit up as I entered her room, and she reached for me to grab her. I picked her up and twirled her around as I danced a waltz around the room. I felt nothing but love in that moment. I felt free in that moment. I felt God in that moment. This is how I was supposed to feel daily. I was supposed to enjoy the beautiful bundle of blessings God gave me. I wasn't supposed to be stressed out and upset and unable to smile, and unable to provide Sasha with the love and joy and positive energy she deserved.

Men either don't realize or care about how their actions not only influence our behaviors but our mind state as well. They don't consider how hard it is to care for a child in a condition of heartbreak.

Heartbreak begins at the very core and essence of you and then spreads to the central nervous system, consuming the mind. And, don't we know all too well how powerful the mind is? Proverbs 23:7 says, *"As a man thinketh in his heart, so is he."* So, essentially the heart controls the mind, and the mind controls not only the body but one's entire existence. Heartbreak is a very different disease for that reason. It is impossible to contain, and the remnants of heartbreak remain with its victim forever. Therefore, it can never be cured, only managed. Yet, a man will inflict us with this disease and expect us to function and continue to nurture and care for their children as if we are immune. I am by no means excluding women as offenders of this particular crime. However, statistically, women are the primary caregivers for the children, and for the sake of this reading, the fact that women do it too is of no consequence.

As previously stated, this state of euphoria felt when with Sasha is where I wanted to exist. Unfortunately, at the time that I had this epiphany, I was still very young, very naïve, and very bitter. So, rather than realize those feelings I felt had nothing to do with man but everything to do with God and His direct reflection of love in my baby's eyes, I gave the credit to Man, specifically, Mister. I will call him Mister for now, because in the thrusts of passion, I failed to retain his name. Mister made me feel like a new woman, or so I thought. Therefore, I acted on this notion, leaning into my own understanding, the only understanding I was aware of, as God was still somewhat a foreign concept to me.

After playing with my daughter, I retrieved Mister's phone number from my secret place, in hopes a name was attached. There, it was! As the mystery unfolded, I let out a sigh of relief. I really did not want to have an awkward conversation with anyone, including my girls, in which I confessed to not knowing the name of the person whom I had just screwed the night before.

I washed and dressed Sasha and then myself. I packed her things up and let Aaron know I wouldn't be back till late. I was headed to Bobbie's house for dinner. She should be home from church, and it was nothing to get her to cook. Just say the word, and she was on it! I didn't contact the rest of the crew cause she and I had some things to discuss. Bobbie was doing her own thing when I was doing mine, and she was not yet privy to my little romp under the stars. I was eager to share.

I rang the bell. Bobbie quickly opened and snatched Sasha out of my hands. This was the routine with us. I wouldn't even be acknowledged for a good 20 minutes until she was done welcoming her goddaughter. She finally came up for air and sat Sasha down in the family room on a blanket with her toys.

"What's up, girl?" she said as she joined me at the table with rolling materials and weed in hand.

I asked her was Rashawn home before I proceeded to spill the tea. He was not. So, the tea party began. Bobbie's jaw dropped as I told her what took place. She was shocked that it happened and appalled she didn't get to see him. She couldn't concentrate on her task at hand. I had to finish rolling the joint while telling the rest of the story.

We stepped just outside the family room onto the patio to smoke and to continue our conversation. I wasn't sure how Bobbie would react to what I had shared with her, but I had a pretty good idea and was spot on. Bobbie's reaction to what she heard was one of mixed emotions. Bobbie hated Aaron with a passion. Sure, she had been cordial for the sake of Sasha, but I always knew how she really felt. So, on the one hand, she was happy that I'd entertained someone else and allowed myself to feel good. She was also pleased with the fact that Mister put it down. I mean, think about it! It's a terrible thing to risk it all for something that wasn't worth the introduction, let alone the act. Luckily, that was not the case in this situation. The reward didn't necessarily outweigh the risk, but it made the risk alright with me.

On the flip side, Bobbie did not believe what I had done was wise. She encouraged me to bite the bullet and tell Aaron we were over. She was so afraid of what would happen if he found out what I had done. Bobbie dang near lost her mind when I shared my truth in that I wanted to do it again and needed her to watch Sasha while I did.

Bobbie was never going to say no to watching Sasha, despite not liking the reason behind the request. Her issues with what I was doing were not because of Aaron, but because of her own lived experiences as well as mine. I believe I mentioned early on that she had been a victim of domestic abuse, but not directly, per se. Her dad used to hit her mom, and her sister showed up on her grandmother's doorstep one day beaten and bloody, courtesy of her baby's father. Bobbie was shell shocked by the things she had witnessed. She knew what Aaron was capable of, and she did not want to see anything happen to me. She begged me to chill out and just break up with Aaron, but I was all in. I liked the thrill.

"Thank you! Love you! I'll be careful," was what I shouted as I head out the door.

* * *

I had fallen into a coma after Mister put it down on me. Good dick will do that to you. When I finally woke up, I was in a strange home, in a strange bed. I pulled back the curtain to daylight and realized I had stayed out all night. I quickly jumped to my feet and put on my clothes.

So many things rushed through my head as I scrambled to get to my phone. My phone must have rung a million times judging from the number of missed calls. Yet, I never heard the phone ring once. Bobbie was one of the frequent callers, of course. I dialed her number with the quickness, and before her phone could ring, she answered. She told me Aaron called her at least a dozen times, but she never answered. To her knowledge, he hadn't shown up to her apartment. So, she and I decided, the best thing would be to say Sasha and I had fallen asleep. I woke up late for work. So, rather than tussle with Sasha, Bobbie would keep her. I would just run home, change and go to work. We just fell asleep, no harm, no foul. That was the story.

As I approached my house, my stomach knotted up. I was so scared. At first glance, everything looked ok. The lights were off, and I hoped Aaron was still asleep.

I opened the door slowly and made my way in.

Before I could get to the stairs, I heard a voice say, "Where is my daughter?" I turned to find Aaron wide-awake, sitting on a chair in our living room.

"Oh, hey, she's with Bobbie," I replied. "We smoked too much and passed out last night. When I woke up running late for work this morning, Bobbie volunteered to keep her. She said we could pick her up whenever." I turned from him and started up the stairs, hoping that the answer would suffice.

Yeah, Right! It didn't.

Aaron grabbed me by my hair and snatched me back down the stairs.

"You a lying bitch!" he hollered. "I know where you were! You were out fucking that nigga KT! You thought I didn't know? Your dumbass thought you was gone get away with it!"

As he continued to berate me, his grip on my hair got tighter. I swear, I thought I would be bald in just a matter of seconds. I thought I wanted him to let go, but when he did, I wished he hadn't. He let go to grab my throat, and he started choking me. I was powerless. He was going to kill me. He choked me until my limbs went limp. He let me go, and I dropped to the floor.

"Nah, bitch!" he shouted. "I can't kill you. My daughter would never forgive me." He grabbed me by my hair again and pulled me to my feet. He slapped me, and I fell to the floor. He stood over me and repeatedly punched me until I blacked out.

* * *

When I came to, I slowly raised up. I was disoriented, and I was in so much pain. There was blood everywhere. I started crying.

"Where is Sasha?"

"She's with Bobbie where you left her. Remember!"

"I need to go get her!"

"Bitch, you ain't going nowhere! Get your ass in that bathroom and clean up! I'm tired of looking at your ugly ass!"

I could hardly move.

"Aaron, I need to go to the hospital."

He grabbed me and dragged me into the bathroom and said," Here's your hospital," as he slammed the door.

I took hold of the sink and pulled myself to my feet. I had two black eyes. My mouth was busted. My neck had fingerprints and whelps from where he choked me. I had bruises everywhere! I couldn't believe I was still breathing. I had to get away from him.

I ran the shower and just sat in the tub as I didn't have the strength to stand. The water helped me recoup some of my senses. I replayed the day prior to the blackout in my mind. I realized I was supposed to be at work, and I was supposed to get a check that day. I knew if anything could get me out of the situation, money could.

I told Aaron I needed to go to work to get my check. We had bills due, and since I was the only one working, my check was important.

"I'll drive you to work to get your check. You are not going nowhere without me," he replied.

I found a pair of sunglasses to hide some of the damage he had done and to make him feel comfortable enough to let me walk in by myself. I arrived at the department store where I worked, pulled the manager to the back, and removed my shades to expose the damage this man had done to me. My manager called security and the police and had Aaron arrested. She told me to take a few days off, my job would still be there, and handed me my check.

I headed over to Bobbie's to get Sasha, grateful that I was still alive. Bobbie opened the door. The shades didn't keep her from seeing what Aaron had done to me. Tears started pouring down her face. I believe in that moment I was gazing into the eyes of that five-year-old little girl that opened her grandmother's door to see her big sister being held at knifepoint. I was sorry I did that to her. I wouldn't do that to my daughter. I was done with Aaron.

Chapter 13: Letting Go

Letting go is hard. You find that out the moment you try. Even harder is letting go when you don't have a relationship with the one being that can comfort you through it all. *But the Comforter, which is the Holy Ghost, whom the Father will send in my name, he shall teach you all things, and bring all things to your remembrance, whatsoever I have said unto you.* (John 14:26)

After the beating, I moved. I moved to an apartment in the south side of Clifton. It was a very liberal community, consisting mostly of people with "alternative lifestyles." In other words, I became a part of the LGBT community, but only as it pertains to the physical location, not physical acts.

It was cool living on my own. Remember! This was my first time. When I left the nest, I moved to the dorms but stayed in Aaron's. When I left school to have my daughter, I moved back into my parents' home. Upon return to Cincinnati, I moved back in with Aaron. Living the single life was a new, exciting adventure for me, and the community in which I lived, made it even better.

My neighbors in the LGBT community welcomed me with open arms. They embraced me, and after finding out what I'd been through, protected me. Thank God they did. See, Aaron was only locked up for 30 days behind what he did to me. His football coaches made sure of that. They did their due diligence to get Aaron out of jail. It's a shame their due diligence stopped there. He wasn't suspended. He did not have to sit out of one game despite his criminal act. He was not forced or even encouraged to take anger management classes, seek counseling, or anything of the sort. Therefore, about a month after his release, the harassment commenced.

I thought I had done a good job keeping my whereabouts a secret. Only my closest friends knew where I lived — my closest friends, and Mister, that is. Yes, the relationship I started, to get even with Aaron, was still going on. I was giving Mister a shot at the title, but unbeknownst to me, Mister already had a championship belt. He just removed it when around me. What I mean by that is, Mister had a girlfriend, well maybe not a whole girlfriend, but close enough.

Mister was involved with a chick from UC's dance team. Now, I didn't know this girl existed, but she knew me. Guess how she knew me! You don't have to be a rocket scientist to figure this twist. Mister's chick knew me through Aaron. It turns out she had a type, as well. We had that in common. Ironic as this may sound, the father of my child and Mister's girlfriend had been messing around for several months, long before Mister and I started. From the time she began messing with Aaron, she was checking for me. If she saw me out with my girls, she could go sneak around with my dude without fear of a pop-up.

I don't exactly know when girlfriend discovered I was messing with Mister, but I do know despite her own dirt, it infuriated her. She was the one reporting everything back to Aaron. She was the reason Aaron knew I was with Mister and not Bobbie, the night everything went down. Aaron was not Columbo, his side hoe was. His side hoe was mad at his main hoe and snitched.

One might think that the abuse I had already suffered at the hands of Aaron was enough punishment for messing with a guy who, as far as I knew, did not have a girlfriend. But, no, that was not enough for this chick. She wanted me to suffer more for a crime that I did not know I had committed. So, after following Mister to my house one day, she gave Aaron my address, notwithstanding knowing what he had done to me and would probably do again.

I was angry with this chick for some time. I questioned, as a female, why she would willingly disclose my whereabouts, knowing full well what he had done to me. Where was the empathy?

In retrospect, empathy was probably too much for me to expect of a kid. Sure, we were of age, but we were still kids. She probably didn't understand or care to understand the magnitude of what she'd done. Then again, perhaps age had nothing to do with the matter at hand. Who knows? Maybe, Aaron and Mister were alike in more ways than just their physical appearance. Maybe girlfriend accepted an ass whippin' here or there and didn't see it as a big deal.

The point is, now that I am grown and have lived a bit, I understand a story, like a coin, has two sides. Personal beliefs and perceptions drive people's reactions to situations and behaviors. I will never understand why she would do such a thing because I don't have the capacity to do it. Then again, I understand love makes you do crazy things, but I digress.

Aaron knew where I lived, and just about every day that I returned home with Sasha, a neighbor had a story about him creeping around my building. Then, I would find flowers at my apartment door, as well as love notes saying how he'd changed and wanted his family back. I would continue to probe the neighbors and get an account of the car he was in and who was driving. Often, the driver was a female with a description fitting that of Mister's girlfriend. The other description sounded a lot like Terri. I don't know what kind of chick takes a man she is dealing with to another woman's house to make up or to harass her or for any reason. Leave it to Aaron to find not just one, but two of those unicorns.

Aaron started showing up to my apartment so frequently that he began to worry my neighbors. He began to exhibit signs of a full-fledged stalker. My only saving grace was my knowledge of his football schedule and me being able to work the shifts I wanted at work. This kept him at bay until it didn't.

One night Aaron came knocking, and I was home. He must have been outside waiting me out because he knew I was there despite me hitting light switches and crawling on the ground like he was a Jehovah's Witness. He banged on the door, demanding that I let him in. He woke Sasha with all the noise, and she was terrified. I kept telling him to leave. He wouldn't. My neighbors started turning on lights and coming out of their apartments with phones in hand, threatening to call the police. They let him know they'd recorded every unwelcomed visit. They were on it and remained until he finally left. Like I said before, I loved my neighbors. They protected me.

Aaron never showed up at the apartment again. Instead, he started showing up at my job. I would call the cops, and by the time they showed, he would be gone, so they didn't have grounds to lock him up. He continued with this routine for about a month. My managers tried to be understanding, but it just came to be too much. He would show up, causing a scene, frightening the customers. Then when the police showed up, I was pulled from the floor to give my report. I became a liability to my company because of the things I was going through. His antics cost me my job. After that, I realized the only way I would have peace and the ability to move on with my life was if I left Cincinnati and went back home to Jersey. I didn't want to, but I had to. I had to get away from the violence and the love triangles and the chaos. I had to take control of my life.

Chapter 14: My Man

Upon my final return home to New Jersey, I found that even family wasn't enough to fill the void of a man, and especially not my man, Aaron. Yes, I said Aaron, not Mister. I mean. In the spirit of keeping it 100, Mister was a rebound. I wasn't over Aaron. Despite my efforts, I had never had the opportunity to break away from Aaron. He consumed my thoughts with his antics and constant abuse, but believe you me I was determined to do so with him 700 miles away.

I had a child, but my parents were so in love with Sasha that I could come and go as I pleased. So, I did. I was on my mission to be Aaron free.

I linked up with my Jersey girls, and we kicked it. I lived in my 20s. We would frequent all the spots the celebrities frequented, so we were at all the New York block parties. We enjoyed the "underground" club scenes. We partied like rock stars.

* * *

I was at an all-time high when Aaron rolled back into town, which was about 18 months after my return. We didn't hook up. We were not a couple. In fact, I was booed up. I pretended Aaron was a non-factor. You know that saying fake it till you make it. That was me all day every day. I kept tabs on him on the low, but on the surface, I was on cloud nine with my new thang.

My new thang was a "nice" guy. He wasn't what I'm used to dating. He wasn't buff and rough. He was a bit on the preppy side, very clean cut. He had a little money, was generous, and presented himself as this upstanding guy. He was such a far cry from Aaron, I thought surely, he'll act like he has some sense, but the fun lasted until it didn't. About six months in, I realized I was wrong!! I had been bamboozled, led astray. My new thang was just as bad as Aaron. Every time we went out, he would end up disappearing. I'd see him consoling, explaining something to some chick before making his way back to me. His story was always the same. *"That's my boy's ex. She's like my little sister. She saw him in here with someone and just got upset. I wanted to make sure she was alright."* I fell for that bull every day until I stopped. The day he came to get me with a busted headlight was the final straw for me. When asked what happened, the story he gave was that his boy was driving his car with some random girl in it when he saw his actual girlfriend. His girlfriend saw the two of them and allegedly went ballistic.

"Yeah, ok," I said.

Unbeknownst to him, I had already done my research. I knew the light was busted and by whom, before he pulled up with this lame excuse. Needless to say, the busted headlight had nothing to do with his boy, and I kicked him to the curb that day.

The next guy I messed with was ugly, with money. I thought surely he knows he's not even supposed to be with me. I brought his stock way up, or so I believed. I was surprised to find an ugly dude can stretch his dollar just as long as a pretty one, with regard to managing thirst. This dude had a whole gang of tricks on standby, each one badder than the other. He was so sure of himself that he would have other women approach him with me there, give them a knot to spend, and send them on their way. He would tell me, *"That's just my friend."* Biz Markie had already warned us about "just a friend." That line was my queue to exit stage left.

Neither of those relationships lasted longer than ten months. Both were as bad, if not worse than Aaron.

I understood, at that point, all men were dogs. If I were going to be subjected to these doggish behaviors, it would be from my baby's daddy, not someone else's. So, Aaron and I started messing around again. Only, this time was different. Aaron was seeing other people, and I was seeing other people, but I was only sexing him. It was convenient for both our situations. He had to be a part of his daughter's life, right? So, when an inquiring mind wanted to know what was up with us, the answer was Sasha. That ended the conversation.

Although I was still messing with Aaron, I'd hoped someone would sweep me off my feet, making it possible for me to move on from him, once and for all. Unfortunately, the exact opposite happened.

Aaron had spent years trying to poison his sister against me. He wanted an ally when he and I were at war. He started vicious rumors about me being with her boyfriend, and he told her I talked bad about her behind her back. He put forth countless efforts to destroy our relationship, but all were futile. Aaron's sister loved me. She loved me so much that when she said, “I do”, she asked me to be in her wedding. I loved her too, so I graciously accepted.

Aaron didn’t have a problem with me being in the wedding. We were in a good space. Aaron's girlfriend, on the other hand, was livid. She wanted him to bow out of the wedding, because I was in it. When Aaron's sister got wind of that, she decided to really piss his girl off. She paired us up. We had to walk down the aisle together, exit together, dance together, and sit at the wedding party table together. For the duration of that wedding, Aaron looked at me like I was the only woman in the room. As for me, I only had eyes for him to begin with. By the end of the night, Aaron's girlfriend was history, and he and I were back in stride again. I was his first lady.

* * *

Aaron moved in with me that following weekend. I was on a cloud. Seeing him interact with Sasha and having him in the home as our protector gave me so much joy. That joy lasted every bit of two weeks. I remember it like yesterday. I was washing dishes preparing to cook when I heard a knock at the door. I peep out, and Aaron's ex was knocking at my door.

I was always taught to strike first. So, when I realized who was at my door, I grabbed a blade. I didn’t know what that girl wanted, but I knew she wasn’t there to play nice. She was not about to catch me slipping. She was there to start shit, and I was ready to finish whatever shit she started. I opened the door slowly.

“What do you want? Why would you think it's ok for you to knock on my door?”

She replied, “I’m pregnant” and walked away.

Now! If that isn’t a mic drop, I don’t know what is. I was completely devastated. I felt like God reached in my chest and snatched all the air out my lungs. I was completely crushed. I shut the door and turned to find the room behind me, spinning. I fell to the floor on my hands and knees and just started crying. He gave another woman his seed. He gave another woman his seed. He gave another woman his seed. In my best Florida Evans voice, I shouted, “Damn! Damn! Damn!!!”

Chapter 15: New Kid In Town

I wasn't ready for the information I received. However, once the initial shock wore off, oddly enough, I was somewhat relieved. I knew Aaron wanted a boy, and I knew I did not want any more kids. I knew she was his girlfriend at the time she got pregnant, so in that case, he hadn't cheated. Yes, the idea took some getting used to. I was no longer special in that regard. I was no longer his only "baby mama," but so what? I couldn't be with a man who didn't take care of his kids. Nor, would I ever come between a man and his child. With that being said, I could do two things. The first being accept the fact that Aaron was having another child, and not by me. The second was to be grateful that I was free from having to subject my body to that pain again since it was the boy he wanted. Besides, Sasha was a miracle baby. I probably couldn't have another child, even if I wanted to.

* * *

November rolled around, and with that, a new addition to our "makeshift" family. I was in love the minute I laid eyes on Aaron's baby boy. How could I not be? He was sweet and innocent. He looked just like the loves of my life — his sister and his dad. I would love him like my own.

The baby spent a great deal of time with us. I appreciated that his mom did not play games, forcing Aaron to her house to see him, or worse, withholding visitation rights. Over time, we became quite cordial. I now had five years of practice being a mom, whereas she was just getting acclimated. I believe she appreciated the support and the breaks. I did consider the idea that Aaron and his baby's mom were still messing around and concluded this was most likely the case. That conclusion did not bother me. I expected as much. A man who did not continue having sex with his baby mama was a unicorn in my world. As long as she was respectful, and I was uninformed, I was not losing sleep. In fact, I slept great until I could no longer.

Now, I know what you're thinking, and you're correct. I stopped sleeping because of baby mama drama, but you'll never guess who the baby mama was. This time, it was me! I found out within two months of the birth of Aaron's son that I too would be having a child. I didn't need a sonogram to tell me what I was having, either. My body told me everything my conscious mind was unaware of or at least pretended to be. Number one, I could have babies; number two, I wanted Aaron's namesake; and number three, I was having a boy. Boys carry on the name. I do not know a man who doesn't want that. To have another woman give Aaron the son he wanted, clearly did not work for me. I was going to give him a son.

I was a little apprehensive about telling Aaron what I believed to be great news. I was afraid he wouldn't feel the same. I don't really know why I felt he would be angry. I just did. Unfortunately, my intuition was spot on. When I finally let him know, Aaron was not happy at all. In fact, he looked me in my eyes and said the baby was not his. This response perplexed me. Where was the man that swept me off my feet at his sister's wedding? Where was the man who was so grateful to me for accepting his baby as my own? Truth be told, I think he was feeling guilty and out of order for having a baby by another woman. You know that's the point of no return. So, when a man comes back from that, they worry you are going to be on some get back, some revenge.

Once Aaron found out about my pregnancy, he began acting stranger than usual. He was so paranoid and insecure. He was short and crass. He started hanging out in the wee hours of the night, reverting to his college days. He wasn't having sex with me. We weren't speaking except when he needed something for his restaurant endeavors. Despite the mental and emotional abuse, I justified helping him start his restaurant because it would ultimately help my children. So, I continued to be everything he needed, for him, while he commenced to be nothing, I needed him to be. This made my pregnancy very difficult, and I was extremely depressed. I was mentally and emotionally exhausted. I was physically drained, taking care of Sasha, wearing the mask that grins and lies, for appearance's sake, all while dying inside. It was too much to bear. I knew I had to do something, or my unborn child would not make it to term.

I remember lying on the couch one night, with tears rolling down my cheeks. My daughter then comes into the living room and says, "Mama, can you help me pray?" She caught me off guard.

This was not routine in my house, but what's that the Bible says? "*A little child shall lead them...*" I'm so glad.

I didn't talk to God a lot, but I realized the moment my baby asked to pray that I needed to. I didn't know what exactly provoked my daughter to ask for help praying. I didn't even ask. I just did what she asked. I went into my baby's room. I grabbed her hand, and together we kneeled at the foot of her bed.

I looked at Sasha and said, "What do you want to pray for?"

She replied, "You, mommy!"

My second encounter with God was as unique as the first and came by way of the same vessel, my baby girl.

"Ok, baby. Praying just means you are talking to God, so tell God whatever you want to tell Him, and He will hear you."

"God, my mommy is sad. I don't want her to be sad. Please, make her happy again."

"Is that it, baby?"

"Yes, mommy!"

"Say, Amen."

"Amen!"

I turned to my baby, and I let her know. "God gave me you, and nothing makes me happier than that. Every time I look in your eyes, I'm happy again. Mommy is just emotional with the baby. I'm ok, though. I'm happy." I threw Sasha on the bed, tickling her, before tucking her in and kissing her goodnight.

I lingered long enough to watch my baby drift off to sleep. I crept back to my room and climbed in my bed. I positioned myself on my back, as the discomfort of carrying a whole other human inside me left me limited options for comfortability.

As I stared at the ceiling, I began to talk to God.

The first thing I said was, "Thank you." I thanked Him for speaking through my child and welcoming me to come to Him at a time when I did not think I had a friend. I thanked Him for forcing me to focus on my blessings. My daughter was a blessing that brought and continues to bring me great joy. My unborn child was a blessing. Aaron was nowhere near as precious to me as my children. Yet, I allowed him to steal the joy that he didn't give me and shouldn't have been able to take away. I let him steal a joy that should have been reserved for my daughter. Instead, she saw my hurt and pain and began to assume some of that hurt and pain.

See, we as women don't always realize the impact that toxic relationships have on us and how much it affects our day-to-day operations. Those unhealthy relationships often make us mismanage the healthy ones. When a person upsets you to the point where you can't be what your kids need you to be or where you can't perform the way your employer requires you to perform, or where you can't love yourself the way you deserve to be loved, then you must reevaluate that relationship. Ask yourself is that toxin worth damaging every other vital, healthy bond in your life? Very rarely will the answer to that question be yes. Who is worth that besides the one that came out of you? And even that gets old at some point. Why was I allowing this man to take so much of me while getting nothing in return? I cried out to the Lord, and He heard my plea.

* * *

In October 2001, I had a beautiful bouncing baby boy who looked nothing like me, and exactly like his father. For me, this fact was bittersweet. Aaron really didn't deserve to have another replica of himself running around after the way he'd treated me. At the same time, I took great pleasure in knowing he couldn't deny this boy without his conscience guilting him to death. I did not expect an apology from him. Humility was not his strong suit, but I knew that he knew, he was dead wrong. That was enough.

The next couple of years for me with regard to Aaron were simply a matter of motion — me going through the motions with little emotion involved. I was in love with my kids. I didn't have time to deal with Aaron's nonsense.

Despite Aaron's success with the restaurant that I helped him start, and despite Aaron being in the same house with his children and me, he offered very little in terms of support. He did the absolute bare minimum when caring for his children and the maximum to hurt me. Yet, I continued to allow him inside at will — inside my home, inside my bed, and inside of me. He continued to disrespect my home by coming in all hours of the night, morning, or not at all. He started having sex with me again after I birthed his male twin from my womb. Nonetheless, he continued to disrespect my bed, jumping from mine to another one and another one. Oh! You thought

DJ Khaled coined the phrase, “Another one.”? Oh, No! Aaron did that. He continued to disrespect me, continually accusing me of being with other men, berating me day in and day out. Still, his behavior didn’t faze me. I was happy, and he could not understand how I could be happy and unbothered by his behavior. He wanted a reaction that I refused to give him. He was bothered by the emotionless motion and the joy from within that I was now able to sustain. So, naturally, Aaron attributed my contentment to another man and or men.

I must admit that Aaron was correct in his assumptions. I did have another man in my life. That man was bigger, stronger, and faster. He never left my side. He loved me unconditionally, flaws and all. He expected nothing of me but my heart. I had run from this man for so many years because I felt so unworthy. What a wonderful feeling it was to discover he had been waiting for me all along and was ready and willing to accept me with open arms, as is. He knew me better than I knew myself and loved me anyway.

He and I grew closer and closer in Aaron’s absence. I felt a connection with Him, unlike any other. I remember speaking to Him one day when suddenly, something came over me. My body became increasingly hot. I began sweating profusely. I started shouting as tears came pouring from my eyes. It was orgasmic but in the purest sense. He was my Father, my comforter, my protector, my provider. I was so glad He saw fit to come into my life despite my reluctance. He was my number one — that is until Aaron needed me, again.

* * *

Aaron's mom died suddenly in 2002. She was believed to be in good health at the time. No one expected her demise. She just passed one night in her sleep. This tremendous loss devastated everyone, but Aaron literally almost died. Aaron took the death of his mother extremely hard, and understandably so. He fell into a deep depression that only his kids and I could bring him out of, so that is what we did. We supported him through it. We helped him smile on days he wanted to die. I kept his affairs in order. I made him eat. I waited on him hand and foot until he was able to do for himself again. By the end of the year, we were exclusive again, and the relationship I was working on fell by the wayside. The tables turned. Aaron and my kids had my full attention. God got the motions.

Chapter 16: Another One

Our first family vacation took place about a year after we reunited. We had an amazing time at Disney World with our children. We felt like a real "normal" family. Aaron was much better. I was making great money at my job, and the restaurant was doing well. Life was good. I was happy. I had what and who I thought I wanted. In February 2005, I made a deposit on our next vacation to Mexico. I was so excited to take my kids out of the country. This was the kind of life I wanted for my children. The day after making that deposit, I found out I would be taking more children than I thought. I was pregnant, AGAIN!

I felt like Aaron would take this news and handle this pregnancy much differently than the last, considering all we had been through the previous year. I was right. He reacted to the news as I had hoped. He was happy. He got on one knee and kissed my stomach. He told me he loved me and how happy he was that we were growing our family. Then, a couple of months shy of our trip to Mexico, I found out about his sidepiece. Yep! Another one! I don't know why, but I couldn't believe it! Or, maybe I didn't want to believe it. He did this to me, again, and at the worst time. This man did not consider how this could affect my pregnancy. He cared nothing about my wellbeing, the wellbeing of his unborn child, or his children. He was a selfish bastard who would never change. And, here I was having a third child by this selfish bastard.

I quickly learned that the chick he was messing around with knew about me all along. She knew about my kids. She knew I was pregnant. She knew where we lived. After dragging all his stuff out my house, and to the curb, I went looking for her, pregnant and all. The blatant disrespect was too much to bear. I know. I know…why get mad at the woman? She wasn't in a relationship with you. While this was true, I found it very hard not to take it personal that a woman willingly participated in cheating and deceiving another woman, especially when there were kids involved. As a woman, did she consider the damage her actions could have on my unborn child? She needed her ass whooped! My girl wouldn't let me do it, though. My girl made me realize neither of them were worth risking my child.

Vacation time came, and I really hadn't seen Aaron since throwing him out of my house. I did not know whether he would show up at the airport. I was torn when he did. That saying absence makes the heart grow fonder always seemed to apply to Aaron. I missed him, and it showed. We had a really good vacation. I think that's why people like vacations. You can escape your real world for a couple of days. I know that's why I love vacation. When we returned home, I didn't want the magic to end, so it didn't.

Aaron and I continued to mend our relationship. He swore to me he was no longer messing with Ronnie. I wanted this to be true, so I chose to believe him. I was about to have his child. I wanted him with me. Two months later, I gave Aaron another son. He was so beautiful. Once again, I was on cloud nine with my babies and my man. Unfortunately, this did not last long. Aaron was back on the prowl just two months after my little man's arrival. He had found someone else to do. What was wrong with me? Why was I not enough?

Maybe, I was overreacting. All men cheat. Why would mine be any different? It's ok. He did not love them. He loved me. He was just screwing those girls. We were cool. No worries, just so long he came home... *Oh! She's pregnant, and she's keeping it?*

Chapter 17: He Who Is Without Sin

I let this information marinate for about a week. Let me rephrase. I internalized what I was feeling for about a week, and then it happened. I exploded. Aaron came in the house one Wednesday night, smelling like sex. Everything I'd been suppressing rose to the surface and manifested itself by way of a woman scorned. I called him everything but a child of God while throwing his belongings out the door. I made my way to the shoes and began chucking them at him with all my might. Aaron, in his altered and disillusioned state, found my antics quite amusing until my aim improved. The Timberland to the face sobered him up quickly. He regrouped, and it was game over.

I remember Aaron grabbing me by the throat and slamming me into the wall. He choked me before slapping me to the ground. He then reciprocated by stomping me and giving me a Timberland to the face. Only, my encounter with Aaron's Timberland rendered me unconscious rather than sober. I blacked out and remembered nothing from that moment. I can't recall what transpired from the blackout to the cops' arrival. However, I found enough evidence upon my return to the land of the living to conclude I would have been dead had the police not intervened. Thank God my kid had the wherewithal to call the cops.

As I lay in the hospital, bloody, I replayed the incidents that took place in my mind. I could not help but feel partially responsible for what Aaron did. I attacked him when he came into the house. He was reacting, not acting. I could not send him to jail for something I had so generously contributed to. I dropped the charges and kept him at bay for some time. I was ending the relationship, but then the woman, no, the chick that was pregnant by Aaron, had a miscarriage.

I believed the miscarriage was a sign from God. He wanted me to forgive Aaron. After all, He said we are to forgive 70 x 7. He wanted me to love and accept Aaron as is. He told us to come as we are, and He wanted me to stop judging him. He said, *"Let he who is without sin, cast the first stone."* He wanted me to stop trying to change Aaron. God said *King David a whoremonger was "a man after His own heart."* If King David, a whoremonger, was a man after God's own heart, then Aaron's behavior was acceptable in God's sight. If that behavior was acceptable in God's sight, then why not mine? Was I greater than God? Who was I to judge, and to impose my will on someone else? I was no one.

God created Aaron the way he was. He knew about Aaron's insatiable appetite for women, and God makes no mistakes. Maybe He made him this way for me. I couldn't get enough of him in the bed. Why was I trying to curb his appetite instead of indulging? This could only make him love me more. Things would be better for us. This epiphany of mine was the beginning of a journey down a rocky, twisted path that I would only venture down for my husband because "that's what God wanted."

* * *

Aaron and I were married on August 1, 2007. We went to the Justice of the Peace and took the plunge. I was so happy. We moved into our new home, my dream home. Week one was bliss. He and I made passionate sex every day. I was impressed with his stamina. He could release and renew in a matter of minutes. I asked him how he was able to cum so many times a day. He said nothing but reached over and extracted a small vial from the drawer. The vial had a small wand with which he scooped out its contents, a white powder. He placed the wand under my nose and said sniff. As I sniffed, some of the powder went in my nose. I quickly snatched away, and he promptly corrected me. “It’s ok,” he said. “Finish it.”

So, I did. The rush was crazy. It was as if I’d been transported to another place. I had no conscience, no inhibitions. I was free. As I floated off into outer space, Aaron laid me down. He took the vial and shook its contents from my belly button to my kitty. He snorted the line, and then he gathered the residue with his tongue. Then he licked and sucked till I exploded on his tongue.

The next week, I thought I’d treat Aaron. I took him to the strip club. I paid for the baddest chick in there to give him a lap dance. As I watched her grind on Aaron’s lap, I became increasingly aroused. This was a good thing, because not only had I intended to treat Aaron at the club, but I also wanted to treat him afterward. The strip club was a way to test the waters before jumping in. I had never done this. Welcoming another woman into our bed sounded good in theory, but I did not know if I could stand to see Aaron with someone else. Furthermore, I did not know if I would want to engage.

As she continued to tease Aaron, burying his face in her breasts, I found myself more and more intrigued. She turned around, bent over, and began making her butt clap. She turned, dropped in a split and started groping his crotch as she slithered back to her feet. Aaron saw the look of fascination on my face and whispered something in her ear. The next thing I knew, she made her way to me. I was leaning against the wall. She began facing me, winding her body like a snake against mine. She turned and touched her toes as she grind on my pelvis. I was soaking wet at this point. She turned back around and placed my hands on her breasts. Yeah, I was ready. I asked her would she be down to ride with us later. She said she got off at two.

* * *

We hung around and waited as the time was almost upon us. I found myself extremely excited. Aaron, myself, and the chick went to a nearby hotel. I told her I knew she probably wanted to shower first. I wasn't about to be playing with funky kitty. After about 15 minutes, Aaron asked that I join her. He stripped me down, walked me to the bathroom, pulled back the curtain, and helped me in. He pulled the chair in there and got comfortable. The chick noticed I seemed a little awkward.

"Have you been with a woman before?"

"No!"

"This is going to be fun. Relax!"

She placed my back against the shower wall and placed my foot up on the tub to prop open my legs. She started sucking on my neck while fondling my breasts. As she worked her way to my nipple with her tongue, she started fingering my pussy. I started to cream. I opened my eyes, staring at Aaron while she worked her way in and out of my orifices. Aaron's soldier was standing at attention and looked longer than ever. I turned the chick around and bent her over. I took hold of her hair and placed her face over his crotch. She opened her mouth, and I bobbed her head up and down on his member. I gave instructions on how to properly suck my husband. I rubbed on her clit from behind and fondled my breasts while watching Aaron go crazy. He pushed her face away. He didn't want to cum. Shortly after, he pulled us out of the shower. He then laid me across the bed, pinning my arms back, and told the chick to eat the cake. I had never experienced something so sensual n my life. She licked and sucked while he sucked on my titties. She licked and sucked while he plucked and pulled his dick in and out of my mouth.

They switched places. Aaron climbed inside me while she sucked on my breasts. He flipped me over put me up on my hands and knees. She slithered underneath and fingered my clit while Aaron fucked the shit out of me. He busted inside me and I busted all over her. This was the best sex I had ever had. What had I gotten myself into?

Chapter 18: Comfort Zone

Shortly after our night with the stripper, things seem to change. As the days went on, Aaron became increasingly paranoid. He started having problems with my family, thinking they were out to get him, particularly my nephew. Aaron's behavior was erratic. I noticed him sniffing coke almost every day. When I'd question him about it, he'd just get angry, deny it, storm out, and stay away most of the night. He would stumble in the house, waking the kids, smelling like pdussy (pu$$y + d!//). He was spiraling out of control.

One night, the kids weren't feeling well. One had caught a bug and passed it to the others. You know how that goes. I had been nursing them all day and night until they finally drifted to sleep. Aaron came in loud and unruly.

I asked him to please quiet down, to which he replied, "My bad." Yet, he didn't simmer down.

Instead, he climbed on top of me trying to kiss on me. I explained to him how tired I was and why, and that I needed a few hours of sleep. He then climbed off me, allowing me to try to rest again. However, before I could return to a state of peace, I heard him say, "I know what will fix that." I then heard him rifle through his pockets, so I opened my eyes to see what was going on. The next I knew, he was on top of me again with that dreadful vial of powder he had retrieved from his coat pocket.

Aaron pulled that wand out with the scoop of powder and attempted to shove it in my face. I slapped it out of his hand and sat up in the bed. I watched in utter disgust as he tried collecting the dust from the floor like a dope fiend. When unsuccessful, he turned to me. Before I could brace myself, Aaron struck me with the back of his hand, knocking me out of bed and to the floor. From there, he began cursing and dragging me across the room. He stomped me in my stomach, which caused me to scream so loud, it woke my kids.

I could hear them yelling from their rooms, "Mommy! Mommy!"

Their terrified voices did not stop his fit of rage. Aaron continued until he looked up and saw that one of my sons had made his way to our room and was standing in the doorway, horrified, trying to gather up enough courage to rescue his mom... from his role model?? Aaron dropped the fist he had drawn back to punch me with. With his head hung low, he grabbed his coat and left. My son rushed to my side crying and asking me, "Why daddy did this to me?" It was at that moment I knew something had to change. I could not have my boys thinking what their father did to me was ok. I couldn't have them learning and emulating such horrible acts. I couldn't have my Sasha taking such ill-treatment from a man. I had to save myself if not for myself, for my children.

I sought counsel from the neighborhood church I occasionally attended, at my daughter's request, but they couldn't help me. They said only I could help me, but failed to tell me how. The one place I thought would offer refuge turned me away. I was so confused and defeated. Rather than continue the search for help, I began to ask more questions that allowed me to stay in the situation I was in.

See, as I reflect while on this journey of healing, I realize that as painful and abusive and tumultuous my relationship with Aaron was, it was comfortable for me. I had convinced myself Aaron wouldn't get so angry and behave the way he did with me if he didn't love me. No matter what he put me through, I wanted his love. He was my first love, and I wanted him to be my last.

Consequently, in that love was my comfort, no matter what it looked or felt like. So, I asked myself questions to sustain the pain, like… Wasn't this what God wanted? I could not get out, right? God frowns upon divorce, right? I was to stay in this madness until God brought about a change in Aaron, His wonders to behold. Puh! I must scoff at myself. I truly convinced myself God was the architect of this disaster, and I was supposed to grin and bear it until He fixed it. Is that really what the Bible says, though?

So often we take bits and pieces from the Bible, extracting only what we want to justify our own will. Rather than look at the Bible as a complete work and really seek the will of the Lord, we do us. I stayed in a horrible marriage by convincing myself God wanted me to, but God was not the architect of my mess. I was. I made my bed, and despite the messiness of it, was content to lay in it. Things would get better. That's what I told myself... The best was yet to come. I just had to keep the faith.

* * *

A couple of years went by, and the best never came. The arguing continued. The drugs continued. Aaron continued to come and go as he pleased. He continued to cheat, but I stayed on the straight and narrow. Despite the turmoil, I continued to perform my duties as his wife. I even did one better. I found myself pregnant by Aaron in April 2009, but I couldn't bring another child into this mess, so I had an abortion without him knowing I was expecting. Now, one might think I would get on birth control of some sort after this ordeal. I mean I was three kids, make that four kids in, counting the abortion. Clearly, what I believed years prior, you know that I couldn't get pregnant, was a myth. I was fertile Myrtle. Yet, even after my abortion, I took no precaution. I continued to have sex with Aaron, with no birth control. Six months after my abortion, I was pregnant again.

As I contemplated aborting this child, God spoke a word to my heart and told me, "No! Trust me! It will be all right." And, so, I gave birth to another beautiful baby girl.

Nivea had the biggest, brightest, most innocent eyes. She was an angel sent from Heaven and made me put things in perspective, once more. I had to take care of me, so that I could take care of my children. I would not continue to allow Aaron to beat me and mistreat me. I had to get off this wreck of a train.

The next time Aaron hit me, I called the police. As a result of his actions, people refrained from doing business with him. He lost contracts and opportunities. Rather than hold himself accountable, he blamed me and refused to work anywhere. He did not contribute one penny to our household. Everything went downhill from there. Aaron officially left his family in shambles, once again. I lost my house. We had to return to my parents' home. To add insult to injury, another woman began harassing me, claiming she was his girl.

I was at the lowest of low and didn't think I could go any lower until on February 12, 2011, my baby boy was diagnosed with Nephrotic Syndrome, and then nothing else mattered.

Chapter 19: Punching Bag

"In children, Nephrotic Syndrome causes these symptoms that include fever, fatigue, irritability, and other signs of infection, loss of appetite, blood in the urine, diarrhea, and high blood pressure…dialysis and possibly a kidney transplant will be required…"

With every word, my heart sank. As the pediatric specialist described to me the kidney disorder with which my son was diagnosed, I checked out. I had an out-of-body experience; one in which I was free from the helpless, powerless shell that life used as a punching bag. As I levitated to a higher plain, I saw my baby clinging to my limp, numb body, terrified of the Boogeyman that had been unleashed to haunt him day and night. I quickly returned from my short-lived journey to the land of the living, where my baby needed me.

"Kids with childhood Nephrotic Syndrome get more infections than usual. The proteins that typically protect them from infection are lost in the urine. They may also have high blood cholesterol. Ms. Marlowe, Nephrotic Syndrome is not curable but is treatable and manageable…" "Doctor, I really wish you had led with that. Bedside Manner is clearly not your strong suit. I pray treatment is. What do I need to do to keep my baby strong, healthy, and happy?"

* * *

The next two years consisted of me traveling back and forth to the hospital with a sick, six-year-old in tow. I had lost my car, and we had no transportation. Aaron was a moot point, so we had to ride the bus to and from the hospital. I remember days on end, sitting in the hospital contemplating, *Is this really my life?*

As I gazed in my sick child's eyes one day, thinking *woe is me*, I realized the answer to my question was, *no*! My life did not belong to me. I had four children who relied on me for everything. My life was theirs until they were older, self-sufficient, and able to manage themselves. I realized that although I was at my breaking point, I could not break. My baby needed me to find strength from somewhere and exhibit that strength like never before. I didn't know where I would draw from, but I had no choice but to do so. I could live with a lot of things. I could fail myself 99 out of 100 times, but my babies were a whole other ball game. I could not fail them once.

This storm once again forced me into the presence of the one being to whom nothing was too big or too small. This storm forced me in the presence of the one who, despite me turning my back on repeatedly, always answered when I called. I was back in the presence of the all mighty God in Heaven as He was the only one who could heal my baby.

I began going to church routinely. I fasted, prayed, and demonstrated a faith that could move mountains. I believed with all my heart that God would deliver my child. My faith was paramount to my baby's recovery. Aside from the weekly trips to the hospital, faith was all I could contribute. If you've not seen your baby suffering, you may not understand. You want, with everything in you, to take the pain away. You wish you could suffer in their place, but you can't. You feel helpless as you watch your baby poked and prodded. You feel powerless as your baby looks at you, longing for you to fix it, and there's no way for you to do that. All I could do was lay it at the altar.

* * *

My baby endured months of tests, observation, and steroid treatment. I remember like yesterday the doctor walking in and telling me after six months of trial and error, that my baby was not responding to the treatment as they'd hoped. There was no significant improvement, and they would have to go back to the drawing board. Oh, did I mention how rare this disease is my baby was diagnosed with? He was essentially a test subject. Upon hearing this news, I felt myself weakening. My knees began to buckle, and I felt the tears welling in my eyes. I regained my composure long enough to excuse myself from the room. I could not cry in front of Chris. If I cried in front of him, he would have lost hope. I leaned in and kissed my baby on the forehead telling him everything would be alright. I told him I had to run down the hall to check on something with the nurse. I stepped out of the room and headed to the hospital chapel. Upon entry, I fell to my knees and began to wail. The steroids were supposed to work, God! Why did the steroids not work? Hadn't my baby suffered enough? Hadn't we endured enough? What more could I do? How much more could I bear?

Amid my cry, a voice penetrated my spirit and said, “This is not your testimony.” I knew then, Chris would be fine.

The following Sunday, I got the kids ready, and we headed to church. I took my entire family to the altar and asked for a special prayer for my baby. The church mother rose to her feet, and she stood by my side.

She grabbed hold of Chris and asked him, “Do you believe God can heal you?” I had never asked my son this question.

As I anxiously awaited his response, I prayed his answer would be a resounding yes. Half the battle on any road to recovery, be it mental, physical, emotional, and/or spiritual, is believing you can be delivered.

I was so glad when he looked Mother Barnes in her face and said, “Yes!” Mother asked that everyone touch and agree. She began to pray over my baby. I felt a covering come over me that I knew emanated from his body. I knew we had more fight to fight, but I knew we would win.

* * *

A few months passed, and the doctors suggested another treatment. The treatment required my son to be hospitalized for ten days. I had to commute to the hospital every day to manage my kids. I was more tired than I had ever been in my life, but I had to be there for all of them. Chris had the most beautiful, positive spirit throughout the process. He would save his dessert and ask for an extra portion, so that every day when I arrived, we could have dessert together. He would say, "Sugar makes us both happy."

Ten days of the back and forth felt more like ten months, but well worth it was the effort and sacrifice. This time, when Chris went into remission, he remained! My baby was delivered! To God be all the glory! Finally, we can rest and focus on getting my eldest graduated. To God be all the glory!

* * *

It was June 2012. Summer was drawing nigh, and we had so much to celebrate. My eldest Sasha graduated high school. My baby Chris was done with his suffering. He no longer had to be a human pincushion. Aaron and I, although separated, were civil toward one another. I was shocked when he said he wanted us to travel to

Jamaica to celebrate. I was definitely in need of a vacation and knew my kids were too. Aaron had no clue what his family had gone through without his support. This experience was hard on everyone but him. So yeah, Jamaica was the least he could do, and I do mean the very least.

I remember arriving in Jamaica being greeted by so many beautiful faces. We pulled up to the hotel, and the highlight of the trip was Chris walking in and saying, “Mommy, I’m in Heaven.” At that moment, I breathed a sigh of relief. I was able to exhale.

Jamaica was an amazing experience for our family. Everyone seemed to be able to reboot. Aaron and I laughed more than we had, maybe ever. A couple of months after our return to the states, Aaron claimed to have had a change of heart. He wanted his family back. Truth be told, I wanted the same. I hadn’t stopped thinking about him since the trip, so I gladly took him back.

Chapter 20: You Had Me At Hello

Aaron and I quickly fell into our groove. The kids were happy. All felt right with the world. I wanted to shout it from a mountaintop. With all the technological advancements that had been made, I had a mountaintop to shout from, Facebook. I began posting every day on social media for all to see. I knew Aaron. Therefore, I knew someone was in the bushes lurking, with no panties on. I couldn't wait to throw our happiness, our family, and us in everyone's face. In retrospect, I probably did not think that all the way through. With all he had put me through, how could I have been so cocky? What reason did I have to have faith in this man, and my ability to satisfy his voracious appetite? I should have known better.

A few weeks after putting our love on display for the world to see, I "inadvertently" received some messages in my inbox that were clearly meant for his eyes only. When would I learn?

Upon reading those messages, I couldn't wait to get home to him. I was getting a divorce. I clocked out of the temp job I was working and saw nothing but red. I made my way home, kicked the door open, and bombed on sight. I slapped him with all my might and demanded a divorce. Aaron responded, but not by yelling at me, or beating me, or even restraining me, for that matter. He responded by taking whatever I had to give, and by baring his soul.

Aaron reassured me the situations I had discovered were old news that had already been dealt with and had been pre-disclosed to me. He literally got on his knees and begged me to forgive him for making me suffer through our son's bout with illness alone. Now, let me pause for a moment. Out of everything that man ever did to me — everything I allowed him to do to me — leaving me to deal with our son alone, hurt me more than all that other hurt combined.

Consequently, out of all the apologies he gave, that apology meant everything to me. You remember in *Jerry McGuire*, the famous line, *"You had me at hello."* Well, that was my "hello." Aaron vowed to honor our marriage, to never cheat again, to protect me rather than hurt me.

I know by now you are like, "Are you kidding me?" I know you're thinking, "Surely, she didn't fall for that. She has to have had enough." Unfortunately, I hadn't had enough. That apology, the apology I had so desperately longed for was all I needed to stay. I disregarded the years of abuse, abandonment, pain, and suffering. I put my rose-colored incorrect-ive lenses back on and stayed in my unsafe haven, not Heaven, haven.

I take this opportunity to draw this distinction between haven and Heaven to make a point. To remain in an unsafe haven, you must choose it over Heaven. The Bible says we will go through the valley of the shadow of death, but we are going through to get to the other side. The valley of the shadow of death is not the destination. Life is and more abundantly. Anything that threatens that the Bible instructs us to turn away from. Yet, we don't. Instead, we use the Bible to justify doing what we want. We use the Bible to stay in our Valley or unsafe haven by way of omission and or partial interpretation of the Word. While not always intended, this process is a clear indication that God is no longer our focal point, once again taking a backseat to every distraction the world has to offer.

More specifically, in my case, I used "God hates divorce," as a means of staying in a marriage that was neither honored by God nor honorable according to the Word. God has made provision for divorce, which were all applicable in my case. So, to stay in that unsafe haven I called a marriage was me completely neglecting God's desire for my life. I find amazing how quickly and easily this choice to turn from God, rather than turn from the valley of death, occurs. Israel did this time and time again and became the first "harlot" to be put away and given her bill of divorce by God. Yet, and still, He received her unto Him again. I think that is why we are so quick to turn because we know God will receive us unto Him again. God is the ultimate rebound guy, at least that's how it has been for me. The minute I would get back with Aaron, I would toss God to the wayside.

You know how we are ladies. We "settle" for the nice guy. We use the nice guy to occupy our time and to be our refuge until the bad boy reenters the picture. You'd think after what I'd been through with my bad boy that I would do better. "Not I," said the pussycat. The minute I accepted Aaron back into my life, so went my "nice guy." I headed left toward the valley of the shadow of death, where all my carnal desires dwelled.

Chapter 21: Devil's Playground

We started frequenting NYC underground sex clubs. My first time was a bit of a culture shock. The space was huge and consisted of a common area surrounded by rooms and booths. The booths had thin curtains you could see through. The rooms had big picture windows with faint red lighting emanating from below. They each had round beds in the center of the room. The entire place was beautifully decorated with Victorian furniture and looked quite upscale. The lights were dimmed. You had to be up close and personal to see who a person was, but you did not have to be close to see everything they were doing. The lighting was perfect in that regard.

Some people chose to wear masks while others did not. Aaron and I wore masks. He thought that appropriate being this was my first time. All around us were free bodies in motion. One would think the smell in there would be horrific, considering what was taking place. To my surprise, it wasn't. I smelled frankincense and jasmine.

While fascinated by the whole scene, it was a lot to take in. I needed a little help to relax. Aaron recognized my discomfort and knew exactly what to do to get me where he wanted me mentally and physically.

I watched as Aaron approached a young lady dressed in all black. Instead of business casual, I would describe her attire as business dominatrix. I had never seen anything like it, but it was very sexy and alluring.

Aaron whispered something in her ear. She disappeared for a moment and returned with a key. Aaron grabbed my hand as we followed her to a vacant red-light room. She unlocked the door, assured us everything had been sterilized and dressed in fresh linens. She instructed us to enjoy and excused herself from the room.

Aaron quickly threw me against the wall. He positioned me facing the picture window, but instead of a window, I saw our reflection in a mirror. Now I knew people could see in just as I had, but I could not see them, which made this experience even more erotic.

Aaron grabbed my neck with one hand gently squeezing as he slid the other hand down my pants. He stroked my clitoris before pulling my panties to the side, plunging his finger in and out, in and out. He removed his hand and sucked the fingers he had entered me with. I was so open and ready for him to do anything to me.

He pulled out his vial and took a hit, all while keeping me pinned to the wall with his pelvis. He dipped the wand in again, this time placing it under my nose. He commanded me to inhale through the nose. I obeyed. Immediately, an overwhelming sensation of euphoria came over me. I felt sexy, invincible, uninhibited. I cared about nothing but the pleasure I wanted in that very moment. Aaron placed the vial on the table next to me and then ripped my shirt from my body. He unbuttoned my pants, and as they fell to the floor, he began sucking my breasts. I felt like I was going to explode. I did explode.

He threw me on the bed and placed a line of powder down the center of my body, leading him to the promised land. He worked his way down my stomach, snorting then tonguing then snorting then tonguing. He made it to his destination, spread my legs apart, hanging them on his shoulders, and began ravishing me. His tongue felt like it had never felt before. I forgot where we were. As I writhed with pleasure, I started begging and pleading for my dick. Having made me cum about three times, he finally stopped torturing me and prepared to give me what I begged for.

He stood in front of me, unzipped his pants, and pulled it out. He took the vial and shook a line of powder on his penis, which I snorted before deep throating his rock-hard member. I swallowed every inch of him before he snatched me up by my hair. He then picked me up and entered me, bouncing me up and down on his dick. I took every inch of him until he exploded inside me throwing me to the bed and collapsing on top. As we lay there, chests heaving, trying to catch our breath, there was a knock on the door. The woman in the business dominatrix attire had returned. She announced her shift had ended, and she was thirsty after a long day's work.

He grabbed her, pulled her to the bed between my legs, grabbed her by her hair as he whispered in her ear, "Tell me how I taste."

She got on her knees and sucked me dry before replying to Aaron, “Delicious!”

Chapter 22: About That Life

"The Life" as we called it, was very addicting until it wasn't. The night I slept with another man, at the request of my husband, was the night The Life lost its luster. See, Aaron believed it would be fun to take down a couple, together. I was content with women, but he insisted. So, against my better judgment, if I may call it that, I consented. Just as I suspected, I shouldn't have. Aside from me hating every minute that stranger was inside me, Aaron became more insecure and paranoid than ever after our sexcapade. He became increasingly angry. He was doing coke like it was going out of style. On top of all that, my father fell sick.

My father was the best man I had ever known. He loved me, unconditionally. Despite his disability, he was strong, fearless, and capable. I couldn't imagine life without him. Yet, I had to.

I remember like yesterday, the day I overheard my baby girl telling my dad, "Papa, you have to eat so that you can be strong."

He smiled and nodded gently, but that was the extent of it. He couldn't do much else. He was tired, and I knew his time was drawing near.

I did everything in my power to make my dad comfortable in his last days and to prepare my family for what was to come, but I wasn't prepared. How does one prepare for a loss so great? When my dad passed, I felt like my world had come to an end. Sure, I put on a smile because I had to be strong for everyone else, but inside, I was dead.

As I planned his funeral, I thought back to simpler times, times when I could climb up on daddy's lap, bury my head in his chest, and watch all the monsters disappear. I thought of times when he was my shoulder to cry on, and times when he would move Heaven and earth to make me happy. How I longed for that feeling once more, but it was gone, forever. My dad was gone forever. My brother was gone forever. Georgie was like a faded picture in a broken glass, a distant memory. We saw each other every other major holiday; and while our kids loved one another, things between us were somewhat estranged. Georgie knew Aaron had been abusive. He couldn't look at him without wanting war, and he was just plain mad at me. He was mad, because I hid the abuse from him all those years, and he was also mad because I took the abuse.

With Bobbie, the case was simple. Out of sight, out of mind best describes what transpired. She'd pop up in New York ever so often. When she did, we would get together as if we speak all the time. The reality, however, was quite the contrary. I find funny how time flies when you're having fun, and even more so when you're not. Before you know, years have passed since you last spoke to the ones you hold dear.

Therefore, all I had left was my Aaron, my coked-out, unfaithful, abusive husband who decided to beat me three days before my dad's funeral. Why do you ask? See, I wanted my dad's wreath to say, "Big G," and because this was a name one of Aaron's boys coined, Aaron felt disrespected. Therefore, he beat me until I conceded an untruth, falsely admitting that I was being disrespectful in my choice of burial wreaths for my father.

There I sat on the front pew at my dad's home going service, hidden behind oversized sunglasses to hide the bruises my beloved left on my face. As I stared at that casket, I didn't hear much in terms of a eulogy or kind farewells, but I heard God's voice saying, *"Choose ye this day whom you will serve."* God revealed to me, in that space, the grave sin I had committed. I made Aaron my god. I put Aaron above all things. I had forgotten Aaron was not the only man left in my life. I still had a Father. I still had a friend in whom I would find comfort if I would just let go and let Him.

I read my Bible, to right the wrong that was revealed to me at my father's home going. I sought God, the God who showed me His face at my daughter's birth, the God who kept me through my son's sickness. I prayed. I went to church. I tried to rekindle that flame, that friendship, and get that old thing back. Yet and still, a numbness exhausted my spirit, and a void so great remained where love once resided that I longed for something or someone to fill it. Thank God, He knew my heart and gave me what I did not know I needed.

* * *

In August 2015, I became a grandmother. Yes, my baby had a baby. I really did not know how to react. My son was a 15-year-old father. I never saw it coming. His girlfriend seemed so innocent. My son was so devoted to sports and school that I didn't realize he was sexually active. I don't even know when he had time to get the girl pregnant. He was involved in so many activities. However, knowing who his father is, I don't know why I dismissed that possibility.

The new addition to our family made me furious and ecstatic at the same time. I felt guilty and angry with myself for not paying closer attention and for not doing a better job of enforcing safe sex. I feared my son had no clue what he had gotten himself into, and I felt largely to blame. I was no longer numb. I felt every bit of this. I am happy to say the more I felt, the more I fell in love with my grandbaby. I became exceedingly grateful for this unexpected bundle of joy that God, by way of irresponsible teens, a preoccupied mom, and a disconnected father, blessed us with. I began to live again.

Things were hard financially, especially with the newest addition to our family. However, my kids and kids' kid made it bearable. I could not fall into defeat with so much love around me, dependent on me. I convinced myself Aaron was an intricate part of our support system. So, I forgave him for what he did to me amid the pain of losing my father, and I welcomed him back into the fold to add stability to our lives. Once again, I was ready to journey down whatever rabbit hole Aaron had chosen for me.

I heard God telling me, "No! Stop! I will provide! You cannot serve two masters. Choose!" I ignored, turned His volume down, chose two masters, and disappeared into the abyss.

Despite church on Sunday and Bible study on Wednesday, Aaron and I re-engaged in our alternative lifestyle, so much so that he did not know how or when to disengage. I remember being at a party for one of Aaron's closest friends, Reggie. They had known each other forever and were like brothers. Aaron went missing for a little while. This did not strike me as odd, because he was cool with everyone at the party. I assumed he was somewhere smoking. I was dancing in the corner, minding my business when suddenly, Reggie's girlfriend approached me. She told me Aaron invited her to leave with us. She was offended and wanted to tell Reggie, but didn't want to ruin his night, or more importantly, their friendship. She gave Aaron the benefit of the doubt, blaming his advancements on alcohol and whatever else he was ingesting. I greatly appreciated that. She insisted that I remove Aaron from the premises, and of course, I expedited her request. I told Aaron I wasn't feeling well and needed to leave the party. He must have suspected the hostess wanted him out of there, as he did not put up a fight.

Aaron and I made our rounds, said our quick goodbyes, and headed to the car. I jumped in the passenger side thinking how we dodged a bullet, literally and figuratively. I reached for my seatbelt, but before I could get my belt fastened, Aaron punched me in my face. He started yelling at me telling me he knew I was clowning him with Reggie. He said he saw me follow Reggie into a room. I was never alone with Reggie in a room. I never went past the living room, where the festivities took place, but I knew arguing was pointless, so I did not want to engage. I opened the door to get out of the car, and he snatched me back in by my hair. He drove off, and as God is my witness, I don't know how we made it home. He had his hands on me more than the wheel. He beat me all the way home. He dragged me out of the car and continued to lay hands on me until he passed out. I'd be dead had he not passed out.

The next day, I was forced to cancel on my baby boy. I was supposed to babysit my grandchild, but I was in so much pain I could not. I do not know who my son was more disgusted with, his dad for beating me, or his mom for staying. I was ashamed and embarrassed. Why would I continue to accept this abuse from this man? Was I willing to die at the hands of this man? Clearly, I was, because he was inside my unresponsive body that night, business as usual.

* * *

A few months passed with no domestic incidents. Aaron and I were cohabitating peacefully for a change. One day, while fondling my breasts, Aaron felt a knot. If I'm being honest, I had felt it before, but ignorance was, and still is bliss. I couldn't fathom facing that dragon at that time, so I didn't. Instead, I buried my head in the sand in hopes it would go away, but it hadn't. I was standing face-to-face with that same dragon, and it was time to fight.

Aaron immediately handed me the phone and made me schedule a mammogram. He demanded he be privy to the results and would not take no for an answer. I recall being so baffled. I could not understand why someone who had inflicted so much pain in my life, would take such an interest in my health. Ironic, huh?

Chapter 23: Walking Dead

My dad's birthday rolled around, and It was harder than I could ever imagine. Not only was that the first time I had to face his special day without him, but the news received on that same day would change my life forever.

I remember being deep in thought, meditating on my father, my earthly father, when the phone rang. As I arose to answer the call, I heard a voice say, "Not unto death, but God be glorified." I took a step closer, and the voice got louder; "Not unto death, but God be glorified." By the time I reached the phone, I already knew what I would hear. The voice on the other end informed me I had stage two breast cancer. I scheduled a time to meet the doctor to discuss treatment before hanging up and sinking back into my dad's old comfy chair. I looked up, and I thought to myself, *I'm going to continue to meditate on my father's life now. I'll deal with this bull, tomorrow.*

I don't know how or when I managed to fall asleep, but I woke up where I remembered leaving off in dad's comfy chair. As I wiped the sleep from my eyes, the tears began to fall. The thought of my children suffering because I left them was more than I could bear. *"Not unto death, but God be glorified,"* resonated in my spirit, but in my mind was anguish, anger, fear, and resentment. I could not fathom why God would do this to me.

Soon, the noise in my mind drowned out the peace in my spirit, and I could not contain myself. I flung chairs. I broke dishes. I fell. I stood. I yelled. I screamed. No one was listening, no one could hear me, and no one could save me.

I tried calling Aaron, but he didn't answer. Finally, I began to pray, and, not a reverent, affirming prayer, but an assertive, aggressive prayer. I want to make that clear, for two reasons.

We forget prayer is not always a rhyme or poem we learned as children. Prayer is not always a psalm or a song. Prayer is not always, "Our Father Who art in Heaven…" Prayer is a talk with God, and I had some words for Him. I wanted…No! I needed to know, "Why Me?"

Secondly, God knows our hearts. Hebrews 4:13 tells us, *Neither is there any creature that is not manifest in His sight: but all things are naked and opened unto the eyes of Him with whom we have to do.* Consequently, what good does one do pretending before God? Had I approached this thing spewing Bible verses out of my mouth like All things work together for good. Those words would have been nothing but lip service that meant nothing to me in that moment, and nothing to Him in that moment. God is the potter, ready to fix our broken pieces. God is the bosom in which He wants us to rest when we are labored and heavy laden. God is the comforter when we need comfort. How can He be these things to us if we are not honest with Him? He allows us that space, and He allows us that grace and says, "Come boldly before the throne." So, that is what I did. I went boldly before the throne. I laid it all on the line. When I was finished, the Holy Spirit said to me, "Call Mama. Not unto death but God be glorified."

At that point, I was bewildered. I could not call my mom and add to her plate. Her plate was full. I knew firsthand no greater pain existed then for a mother to bury a child. With my dad's death so prominent, I couldn't put that thought on her mind. Then I realized God never gives us more than we can endure. I was not to call my mommy. I was to call Mama, and I would be obedient to His will. Funny thing is I don't even recall hearing a ring on the receiving end of my phone call. I just remember my spiritual Mama picking up and saying, "Yes, child?" as if she knew it was me with the news she had been expecting all day.

I told Mama I had stage two cancer. She quickly and fervently rebuked my declaration. She said, "Child, no, you don't!" She said, "Don't allow an unwelcomed guest to move into your home." Then, she began to pray and plead the blood over me. She proclaimed! "By His stripes, you are healed!" "By His stripes, you are healed!"

She made me claim it. I shouted, "By His stripes, I am healed!" "By His stripes, I am healed."

Now, I feel compelled at this juncture to define healed. Healed did not mean the cancer was gone. It didn't mean I would do no chemo. Healed did not mean I would escape the valley of the shadow of death. The definition of healed is the process of making or becoming sound again. 2Timothy 1:6 tells us, "*For God has not given us the spirit of fear but of power and of love and of a sound mind.*" Therefore, healed meant that I could, at this point, lean not unto mine own understanding but instead rest in the fact that All things will work together for good to them who love the Lord. Although I had to walk in the valley, I would fear not. God, my Father was with me, and He wouldn't fail me, no matter the outcome.

My spiritual Mama reminded me who my Father was and how big He was. My Father was bigger than any cancer and bigger than death. She spoke life into me, and I was ready to journey on. God allowed me to grieve, allowed me to be human, allowed me to release, and then cradled me in His arms. Instead of lip service, the words became truth, and I hid them in my heart.

The valley was deep, long, and dark. The mastectomy I had in February 2016 did not free me from cancer. In fact, they opened me up to find the cancer was spreading. So, not only did I lose my breasts, which I was actually good with, anxiously anticipating the replacements, but I would lose my hair too. That, I was not good with at all. I was always taught; my hair was my crown. Was I no longer a queen?

Chemotherapy was literally what I imagine hell to be. The feeling was indescribable. The nausea, the lightheadedness, the dizziness, the disorientation, the extreme lethargy — the whole ordeal was quite surreal. At times I laid in bed, contemplating spoiling my sheets because I was too weak to get up. I wanted to die, but I could not for the sake of my kids. Two weeks past, and I finally felt better, but not for long. I had to walk the green mile again. My dance with chemo was not over.

I underwent chemo for six months to rid my body of the cancer. When I finally completed my last treatment, I could have easily starred on *The Walking Dead* with no makeup. I would avoid mirrors like I was a vampire because my appearance pained me so. I hurt so bad, looking in the mirror and not recognizing the person looking back at me. I hurt so bad seeing my baby girl look at me with such pity.

Chapter 24: Looking For A New Love

A month passed, and I began feeling better. The poison was finally escaping my body. My son's baseball team threw me a pink party in celebration of my victory over cancer. This was a surprise party, and I was so touched that they thought that much of me. That party did something to me. It gave me a much-needed jolt. I had begun to think so little of myself. I had started to lose my drive having been beat down emotionally, physically, mentally. I was tired, but the kindness and appreciation my baseball family showed me that day, put a little gas in my tank. I think we fail to realize the power of kindness and the power of love all too often.

I grew stronger every day and gave God the glory. I started a job at a company called BAI. BAI's mantra was, "Be better today than you were yesterday." I adopted that mantra, and with the organizational culture of BAI, being better was easy. People were friendly and positive and were committed to the betterment of others. So, I received life once again, from an unexpected source.

At home, my kids were finally beginning to relax and feel confident I would be ok. They started smiling more and laughing more. They weren't tiptoeing around me, and they began to exhale. I was relieved to see wonder and innocence creeping back into my babies' faces. No one and nothing breathed life into me like seeing my kids happy.

Things were on the up and up when Aaron decided to bring furniture in our house that was riddled with bed bugs. Of course, my body couldn't withstand such an attack, but I just grinned and bared it. I just wanted peace. I wanted my family to be at peace. How I could think my acceptance of bed bugs would bring me and my family peace is beyond me. As always, I thought I could fix it. I made excuses. I pretended everything would be ok and handled it best I could.

Things progressively worsened, and I remained silent. As if our endurance of bed bugs wasn't enough, Aaron decided to become a dog breeder. He brought ten bulldogs to our home. I swear, coke is a hell of a drug but is no contender in comparison to love. Cocaine had Aaron spinning every which way, out of control, and love had me taking every bit of it.

My kids and I stayed away from the house as much as possible, spending a lot of time outdoors, at games. I was getting exercise, having fun. My hair had grown enough for me to get a super cute haircut. I was beginning to feel like and look like myself again. I continued to rely heavily on Mama for spiritual guidance, and her support really helped me when BAI announced they were selling the company. I did not grow weary or fret. I just trusted God that He would speak to me, and He did.

God and I had a long heart-to-heart. He asked me what I wanted. I told Him. I want to build a community center in Trenton, NJ. I want thriving summer and after school programs that help kids stay safe and off the streets. As we talked, I realized I needed money to do that, money that Bai was not going to give me anyway. That's when God told me what I needed was in my home. My home? Nothing is in my house but bed bugs and dogs. Then I thought back to when Mama said, *"Don't let unwelcomed guests stay in your home."* God was not talking about my house. He was talking about my temple, my body. That is when I knew I had to tell my story, the story I held inside me, and my story would allow me to do everything God purposed me to do.

After that, I really started feeling good about myself and about the direction my life was going. I began looking up again. I held my head high again. I looked in every mirror I passed by. The kids and I were happy despite our living situation. Since Aaron wasn't contributing to that air of happiness, his paranoia came roaring in. The accusations began again. He started a rumor that I was sleeping with his boy and even went so far as to tell his boy's girlfriend. Of course, that was because he wanted to screw her. The girl threatened me too, which I responded by providing my home address and welcoming the challenge. She never showed.

Aaron saw me unmoved by his fraudulent actions. He saw me focused and gathering my thoughts, recording my life on my computer. He did not like that, so he smashed my computer. When he did that, I thought This must have been what Celie from *The Color Purple* felt when she found Mista had stolen her scissors preventing her from working on her craft, keeping her from the one thing that made her happy, and the one thing that gave her peace. I lost it. I started tearing his things to shreds. He called the police and told them I hit him. Get this! The cops took me to jail.

In jail, I meditated and prayed. I witnessed to others. I knew God had me there for a reason. On second thought, God didn't have me there at all. I chose to be there by being unequally yoked. I chose to be there because I would not let go of someone who I knew in my heart was no good for me. I appreciate that through everything, God still found a way to use me for His glory despite me.

Upon my return, I insisted that Aaron and I go to counseling. We started talking to an amazing pastor who did his best, but Aaron refused the wisdom. He was not receptive to anything. He was not coachable. He was not compromising. He continued to accuse me of cheating. He continued to hurt me. He disrespected the pastor and me during sessions. The counseling was pointless, so I gave up.

* * *

As the days went on, I begin walking backwards. I fell into a deep depression. Every time I got close to God, Aaron would find a way to separate us. I take that back. That's not a fair statement. Aaron could only do what I allowed him to. I allowed him to distract me and derail my vision. I allowed the abuse. I allowed him to contaminate my house. I allowed him to put me in the sunken place in which I dwelled. Thank God, I eventually saw a doctor for my depression before I slipped further away. My depression had gotten that bad. I was prescribed an anti-depressant which really helped me turn things back around. I know mental health issues are taboo in the black community, but I sincerely hope that changes. I hope we start checking on our mental, so more lives can be saved, like mine.

I rose from the ashes like a Phoenix and began again, recording my thoughts. My energy was spent focused on the positive. My kids and I began to live again. I thirsted after God. Sure enough, Aaron was triggered. He came home one day arguing and making false accusations. I could not bridle my tongue, nor did I think I should have.

He told me, "Shut the fuck up, or I'll slap the shit out of you."

I kept talking, and he blacked my eye. That was the last time. I packed up my kids. My eldest daughter, Sasha, was working, and she put a deposit down on a place for us. We moved out. That was August 2017.

I would love to tell you I am divorced and being pursued by a God-fearing man who loves me the right way, and that I am taking my time because I am putting me first. I would love to tell you I love Aaron as the father of my children and nothing more and that we no longer deal with each other in the Bible way, as the elders would say. I would love to say all those things, but then, I would be lying. We no longer live together. This is true, but I have not been able to bring myself to file for divorce. I still allow him to enter me from time to time, and we "co-parent." I still use excuses like, "I don't want to work on anything new with anyone. Since I have needs, this is a relationship of convenience. I need him to help me with the kids."

These are the lies I tell myself. I won't lie to you, though. The reality is I wouldn't want either of my daughters to find themselves in this predicament. In fact, I would happily go to jail to keep them from anything remotely close to what I have endured. Furthermore, I would die from a broken heart if any of my sons followed in their dad's footsteps. Yet, if either of these things happened, I would have no one to blame but me; because by staying, I condoned this behavior. By staying, I implied this interaction, and this cohabitation was acceptable. I started a vicious cycle and now must implore that my daughters and sons have the courage and strength to break that cycle.

The first step to recovery is admitting you have a problem.

I have a problem. I have an addiction from which I have yet to be delivered. I'm hopeful seeing this on paper, ingesting this word by word, reliving each horrible scene, will free me. I hope it will free you. If it doesn't, stay on your knees in prayer until your change comes, and your sight is restored. Thank you for allowing me to share my life *Through Blind Eyes*.

Author Bio

Bobbie Michelle Bean is a mother, real estate agent, investor, entrepreneur, public speaker, and author of the new novel *Through Blind Eyes*.

Bobbie writes fiction based on real-life; reconstructed biographies, one might say. Her in-depth understanding of human action is revealed in her debut novel, as she journeys through another woman's life, reenacting the good, the bad, the sexy, and the ugly of it all.

Bobbie received her bachelor's degree from the University of Cincinnati, and her master's from South University, where her focus was Behavioral Science, dealing primarily with human behavior as it relates to society. Her expertise in this area allowed her to run businesses for herself and others successfully, and most recently, to explore the inner thoughts and workings of the multifaceted subjects in her writings.

At the young age of eight, Bobbie realized that she was pretty good at writing when her first submission for publishing, a poem titled *Sometimes He Answers No,* was included in a compilation of poetry which her mom still keeps on the mantle. Life and the pursuit of happiness prevented Bobbie from adding more published work to that mantle. Still, it did not stop Bobbie from writing poems, short stories, music, plays, and putting on entire productions for her church and other community organizations.

When not writing, mothering, entrepreneuring, or public speaking, renaissance woman and Cincinnati native Bobbie Michelle Bean can be found working desperately to shed her stomach; sadly, to no avail. She dances in the rain, sings in the shower, cooks big dinners for her family, and celebrates that she is *Every Woman.* When *every woman* gives voice to *every woman*, you can rest assured it will be good!

Made in the USA
Middletown, DE
17 July 2020